T0303603

It's one thing to have
a beautiful voice. It is
another to
    say yes, Montezuma

Cole Swensen

mind is a form
of taking
it all

Robert Creeley

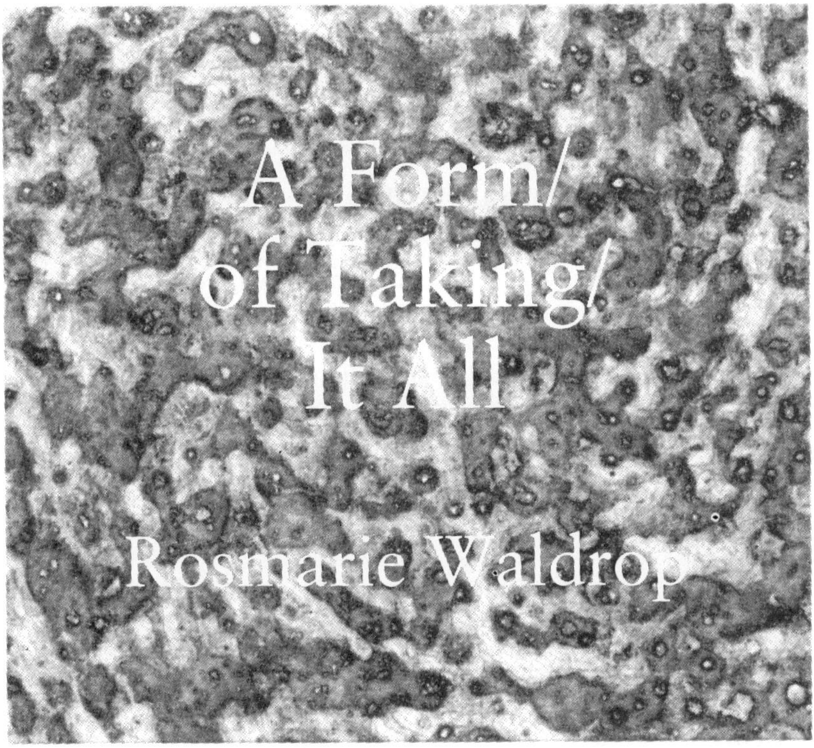

Station Hill Press

Published by Station Hill Press, Inc., Barrytown, New York 12507. Grateful acknowledgement is due to the National Endowment for the Arts, a Federal Agency in Washington, D.C., and the New York State Council on the Arts for partial financial support of this project.

Produced by the Institute for Publishing Arts, Inc., a not-for-profit, tax-exempt organization in Barrytown, New York.

Previously published in *Temblor,* a literary magazine edited by Lee Hickman.

Distributed by The Talman Company, 150 Fifth Avenue, New York, New York 10011.

Designed by Susan Quasha.

Library of Congress Cataloging-in-Publication Data

Waldrop, Rosmarie.
A form/ of taking/ it all / Rosmarie Waldrop.
p. cm.
Bibliography: p.
ISBN 0-88268-092-7.—ISBN 0-88268-091-9 (pbk.)
I. Title.
PS3573.A42345F67 1990
813'.54—dc20 90-11353
CIP

Manufactured in the United States of America.

Contents

I

A Form of Vertigo

The blind is drawn, dark rectangle in a luminous frame. Amy is glad of the clean lines: whenever her eyes do not encounter, her head spins, or is it her stomach, a garden gone to seed, odd costumes among the trees, has she invited Napoleon to shake hands with Montezuma in his feather coat while Columbus throws his coin? Alexander von Humboldt talks twice as fast, and in mixed German, French, Spanish and English. He defends the succession of night and day, but Amy is too dizzy to follow his drift toward the mountains. How long has this been going on?

Any motion once started. The coast clear, abridged version, the plane, Puerta Central Aereo de Mexico, Victoria with the car. Victoria Alvarez Russell. A solemn name for a whirlwind, and curious meter. She remembers trying to joke:

"What a relief, solid ground again. It's not just that I am afraid, which I am, but on the ground you at least see the holes. Those in the air take you unawares. Somebody should paint a ceiling on it."

"You wouldn't be so confident about the ground if you lived here. Remember the earthquake. Volcano country."

Now rumbles inside her, vast subterranean fissures heaving to blast off part of the mountain. The action of a muscle is to contract, and what is to come will come swiftly, glazed volcanic sand and lava stops Cortés' advance.

Victoria slowed down for a bottleneck. "Over there, you can catch a glimpse of Chapultépec Castle, our White House."

Into the cloud of red haze. Traffic, lines knotting and thinning, late complications, lame smile, mopped her forehead as she does now, a voluntary contraction of the fibers in the biceps, not like what has been going on inside her. "I feel queasy."

"It's the *idea* of jet lag," Victoria joked, "even if the flight does not cross any time meridians. People also get diarrhoea on arrival. Before they had a chance to eat an amoeba."

The road bent and straightened just out of phase with the sideways motion in her stomach. Devious. All landmarks disappeared, overexposed. Legs open, head to the left, arms akimbo, "Why did we ever invent planes," she groaned. "Or cars. Too much motion, when already the earth moves."

"How else could we get you here?"

Here. Hot, unfamiliar, trying to squeeze through the four slits around the blind, the slit between the lids. She can of course close her eyes, but the light goes on spiraling inside her head, billowing over the barriers, dimmer, northern sights, fogbound city, smoke stacks, the colder grey, restless, typewriters and schedules, tea water, raincoats, boots. And Ada. Ada watching the smoke coil upward from the tip of her cigarette, her profile sharp against her feathery hair, a bluejay rocks in the tree. Season subtracted, whirled out of reason. The dancing mistress hitches up her plumed skirt so that Columbus sees her legs far above the knees. A telescope on a cliff. She shows him how to walk, how to lift a knee and let the foot touch the ground with the tip of the toes which form a straight line with the shinbone. Only then does she slowly lower her heel. She wears white slippers laced up to her mid-calves and is completely surrounded by a gaseous medium called the atmosphere. A bad omen. Beethoven takes fate by the throat. The messengers leave in great haste for Mexico City where they are painted with chalk and locked up in Cuauhcalco prison. This requires delicate instruments and metrical stress.

She hears water running and music. John's voice from the other side of the wall. Her old friend. And Henry's. More Henry's. Victoria's husband. Twenty years contracted and canceled, muscle over time. She listens, head turned sideways, emphasis demanded by language, lying quite still as if afraid of succumbing to the exertion. Now the voice pauses. She wishes it would continue its rope of pressed plants, volcanic ash, sextants and telescopes, the desire to climb, classify, compare, connect, von Humboldt, no part of his body felt altogether comfortable, and Reinhard, Reinhard. Words to mingle with, a crowd, to feel her body, and when she does.

How long has she been in this room? This house? Victoria's and Henry's, 21 calle Juarez, Mexico City, F.D. The staircase in her head, used by everybody, the wide open air, at great speed, flocks of parrots. And steady syllables, John's: Alexander von Humboldt, his love for Reinhard, how he lifts his field glasses, his desire to climb mountains, his passion for measurement, mapping the cosmos, foghorns and physical description of the universe. But memories along with Humboldt, fever, lunettes d'épreuves, including lean into the past like a drunk? A fork in the road. Henry. What a disaster if they had married. Curing stingray bites by having a prostitute urinate into the wound. It leads to a particularly virulent form of syphilis. Does forgetting count as forgiveness or just being forty, holding her face up to the sun? Now that John's voice has revived the amputated nerve she feels a remote fury in her muscles, things that had not been said, standing alone in front of the door. Stings without landing, it had not only been windy, but raining intermittently. Acrid lies. The track opens onto a black surface of glazed volcanic sand which rises to the perpendicular height of 160 feet, compelling the Conquistadors to take a wide circuit. Cortés sweats in his velvet cloak. At 4:12, two violent tremors knock Alexander von Humboldt's porters to the ground. Nevertheless Humboldt takes out his watch. False move? Has her impatience betrayed her, a muscle, a gland? A dare, as if opposites could not fail to explain, or letters cross without attracting agreement and intimacy. Ada. Her walk. Ada practicing pliés, pushing her hair back like ruffled feathers. Ada sitting as if she could spend her whole life in one position. Ada opening her eyes wide in fits of eager to know, then growing absent, off into a sky of her own, exotic.

Sulfur precipitates on the sides of the crater. Alexander von Humboldt wades through birdlime. With effort he unsticks his sole, lifts his knee and lets his toe touch the viscous mass. The Indians look with fear at the deformed subterranean plants. Columbus sets foot on the Bahamas. Ada in her blue tutu at the first whisper of possibility, when Amy first talked to her, first felt helpless, first caught in a current, too fast, and rocking with fright.

"It isn't just when you dance," she said to Ada whose eyes focused on a thin distance in the mirror, far beyond Amy's reflection, while she tissued the cold cream off her face. "You understand movement in a way that goes beyond muscle, let alone elegant clothes. Whereas I walk too fast."

"Traveling is exhausting," said Ada. Remotely. "I've tired myself out in my blue shoes before even breaking into the spot. Soon I'll only teach."

"If you don't like to travel ..." The sycamore out the window had a single leaf left on it, which fluttered against the street light. Sharp smell of brine, thin smile.

"All the landmarks disappear, the sky heaves all around your eyes. While I was married I dreamed of drowning. A bad omen."

"We all lose ourselves," she replied, then grew afraid, veered off in a rush: "In writing there are no signs for navigation either, not even stars. I throw my coin, a mere adventuress, though with a plan. But words. Mere words."

Went over and over this conversation as if learning a new language, one nearer the bone, a muscle whose action is to contract and thus to bring together the two structures to which it is attached. On her way backstage she stopped at every mailbox. Why had she never noticed their lovely blue? Was it possible? Could a woman whose arms fluttered like wings settle into a house in Boston? She nervously passed the salt. Saw choice slipping out of her hand, into the noise of a machine whose inexorable motion would only stop when it had run full course. "I know how you feel. Though the geological structure of New England is quite simple."

"The weight of the body must be distributed equally over the entire surface of the foot," Ada said. "Only this way can it support the music."

Felt lost, or perhaps only high, looking through a telescope mounted on a cliff, which brings the horizon terribly close.

"Good wine." Ada had looked harassed, which gave Amy hope.

"You've got the deep rhythm," she came out with her excitement. "When you walk even more than when you dance. It must come directly, through the entire surface of the foot, as you say, from the rotation of the earth, this precise, even motion we are part of, which breath and pulse play against. Succession of seasons, of night and day. Even in our sleep, we travel a measurable distance. But I move too fast, the boundaries slide, clouds blow across the sky, the flag moves up and down the mast, and my head spins."

Ada lit a cigarette, her hand darted in short, swift strokes away from her mouth.

Amy's hands are moist. The sheets feel good, fresh and cool against her tiredness. She runs her finger along the fabric, its wrinkles and sharp creases. A fat little girl sits on a chair, buttoned into her coat. Laces her shoes, says thank you, says please, says how do you do. Says 'I.' Fact in her fist, and says it again. Amy points her finger at the child: I know you. I know why you stare at the ceiling. You are waiting for them to fall. The stuccoed fruit, we don't have to say it because we know. She used to think her memory was a cave, but perhaps it is a muscle connected to this child, contracting now, bringing her terribly close. And other shadows, black, white, or taking on color from rubbing her eyes. Moving. Everything's moving. Even the shadows. She can't hold on, can't depend on them. Or words. Words least of all, they blow across the Atlantic or back twenty years, forty, four hundred, through the air, through keyholes like witches. Move with the wind, the rotation of the earth, with heat, with earthquakes, with motor or muscle, with malice.

Never mind Amy, the child. A woman of a certain age, Amy, a certain armor, all cotton turtlenecks. The morning gone, the fire more mineral. And the stillness, the hidden beat she tries to approach with the help of words, mining the intervals between. Fits of effort, finger to the bone, scratching at stone. And afraid of being scattered, matter of worries, jobs, projects, desires, whirling out of control till no place. Keeps at it, obliquely, as if she believed it could only be approached through the maelstrom, the markets, the crowded buses, stores with clerks behind counters, rooms full of children, cats, flowerpots, washing strung up in the yard. Dark center.

The blind would be invisible without the light framing it. She is tired of looking at it, tired of closing her eyes and getting its after-image with the light values reversed, bright center in a dark frame.

The window. The cold room, her breath misting the pane. She had stepped close and written on it: Ada. In triumph. Her finger rested on the pane as if to write more, but the mist had cleared, the word faded.

"This room has the best view," she said. "Not only does it look out on the garden, but the sky is inked to the finest shade pollution can offer."

Ada did not laugh. Stood by the window, her finger tapping against the glass as if preparing to say: a dancer's life is short. Wishing to be alone, perhaps, to think about muscles contracting, sudden dips in the landscape.

A motorcycle had gunned around the corner. They both jumped. It brought them back inside. Ada's face small.

She left her reluctantly. Brim of words in the quick of the throat, wanted to talk all night, drink, smoke, walk in her sleep.

She gets up now and walks the few paces to the armchair. Sees a child peer through the door, disappear. Slick parquet. Strenuous. Breaks out in a sweat. The temperature drooping. Grateful that the chair is cool, a loose rattan weave, its back to the window. No spirit or starch. The past a chemical injected into her body. Infectious.

It is Ada walks in her sleep. Even awake, walks blindly, pulled, as if she saw with her feet. The heel up as if beginning the movement, the toe hardly lifting off the floor. Four viceroys came and went in rapid succession. Columbus traversed every region which up to that time had been navigated. Before daylight, feels her way along walls, doors, leans a long time at the window, runs her fingers along the mullions. Or appears in Amy's room, right foot forward, but can't be touched, stares right back into the air, stares at Amy as at a thing. No way to gauge degrees of awareness, intensity of feeling, possibility of understanding, as she moves her elbows with the odd, fluttering movement she has, or pushes back her hair like a tangle of feathers.

Even now Amy gets sullen, what is Ada looking for, what island with mangroves lining the shore and very great rivers? Something she can't ever know except by its fissures, unintentional vibrations, a sound against the window, trees rocking in the wind, or was it raining?

At least Ada never climbed the roof in the traditional manner, stretching her arms before her to push back the air, keep her balance and a good look-out for land. Carried by a cool wind, the movement begun by the whole extended foot.

"At a certain speed the wheel barely touches the ground," Ada said one night. Was it then that the outlines began to blur, and found the earth pear-shaped, did Columbus, round except where it has a nipple, skin moving in every shadowy twist of Ada's blue robe, legs open, sharp expectancy, as when the first thrill of summer heat turns to thirst, an ache to press against, to fight like sleep, suffocating fatigue.

But enjoyed buttering toast for breakfast, at table with Ada, and voices fused. Squinted into the sun without telescope and asked timidly: your children? your husband? Ada watched the cat chase his tail.

Sits on a cane chair in a house she does not know. Hears steps, voices, a piano stuttering, a child screams, she imagines the rooms bright and sunny, tries to remember John's face, so much less distinct than the voice, her companion. Imagines him at a desk like her own, piled with books and papers, cigars, ashtrays, ashes strewn even so. Bent over his machine, metal movement, magnetic, von Humboldt's sudden desires to describe the universe, climb a volcano, measure the time between earthquakes, wade through birdlime in caves. No part of his body felt altogether comfortable, his face and neck burned, the skin flaking off, every exposed part of his body bitten by insects. She leans forward a little, as if she could stare through the wall and see John's expression as he stops, clicks, lets the rewind purr, listens: "no part of his body felt altogether comfortable," clicks, continues: "but he did not die of yellow fever in Acapulco as had been reported." Her own body feels weak, heavy. Pump creaking. She will lie down again. She knows that the window, should she raise the blind, would open onto a garden of agavas, a hum in the trees, not onto Mount Chimborazo where, high up, a tiny Alexander von Humboldt has trouble breathing, his eyes bloodshot, blood oozing from his gums. Nor onto Pinckney Street where she had stood waiting for Henry and walked, forgetting Henry, in the rain, where Ada is walking now, pulled by the moon or the tides of a piano or simply her feet, but won't talk with the radio on. Makes her edgy, the shadow of noise. Was the lack of answers a beginning of infirmity rather than distraction or closing the lid? Put her arm around Ada who fluttered off to look at a photo on the wall. A small, fat Amy sits buttoned into her coat, stuck into ever larger frames against wallpaper splotched with a steady downpour of wallpaper roses. Works hard at fitting inside the photo, inside her coat, but her legs dangle, a touch of defiance. Between their legs, the young birds had a thick lump of edible fat.

"Speaking with Napoleon: what a battlefield this would make." Paul stuck his hand inside his blazer. "How long have you known my mother?"

Ada made no effort to hide her annoyance. Her knuckles white.

Paul winked at Amy: "whose fault is it if my manners are as uncouth as Beethoven's? With Ada off to rehearsals, practicing *pliés, battements,* or letting her foot touch the ground with the tip of her toes which must form a straight line with her shinbone. Only then she lowers her heel, slowly, so slowly, and stretches her full, round, delicate knee. Yes, I have another question: is there anything to eat?"

So big to have come out of Ada, how much closer to her own shape, a bear, dancing the *minuet à la reine,* a wealth of body to surprise.

Ada's eyes were on the wreaths of smoke swirling up from the cigarette burned down to her fingers. Amy stubbed out her cigar, went over to Ada's chair and began to knead her shoulders, gently digging at the tense muscles to make them untie, knot after knot relaxing and dropping to the floor in big loops.

She felt light, suddenly, as if walking at great speed through the underbrush of thoughts, voices, breaths, conversations, shouts, screams, certain of the clearing. Later, as she showed Paul upstairs, the temptation to set something in motion, even an explosion, some brutal clear violence.

"Napoleon surveyed the locality with a profound air," said Paul dragging his suitcase, then tested the bed. "Nice room, though a bit chilly. You think a lot of my mother, don't you."

She turned the radiator on, surprised to feel her heart beating, the little hollow in her stomach, this desire to make a declaration, dare a lie, simple, unpretentious, to which she could abandon herself with a sudden comfort and nearly call it happy. If she once said: yes, we're lovers, wouldn't it already be closer to true?

She wants to think about Ada. Ada talking of omens. Even though she smiles, and in plain sun, she keeps the halflight of an interior around her. As if standing in a doorway. In an extra layer of clothes. Ada under the same ceiling as Amy the child: why did those fruit never fall? But already she wears a feather coat and fears the Spaniards whose horses carry them on their backs wherever they wish. They come in battle array as conquerors, and the dust rises in whirlwinds on the road. Columbus sets foot on the Bahamas, and the two hemispheres become alike. On top of the Great Pyramid, a captive's heart is torn from his body. She wants to vomit, but the Cabildos depose the Spanish authorities and create provincial juntas. Alexander von Humboldt, using some of his voluntary muscles, parallel striated fibers bound together by connective tissue, puts his arm around Aimé Bonpland who does not look up from his book. Linnaeus: *Species Plantarum*. Napoleon rides over the plain as if carried by a cool wind, the dancer's heels never touch the ground, precarious posture threatened by suffocating sleepiness, the boom of waves relentless, breaking over sand, surf, chique-chiques, spindrift, saliva, which explains why gravitation elongates the watery envelope of the earth very slightly in two opposite directions.

"Maria hasn't called by any chance," she heard Paul ask Ada.

"No. What's going on?"

"You may picture me, like Beethoven, in a turbulent emotional condition: She wants to do some thinking. My guess is that thinking plus distance will overcome cohesion. So, in spite of my age and wisdom, I've run back to my old insecurity blanket—who also keeps suggesting I get out."

"This isn't my house."

"Your Amy doesn't seem to mind. Or don't you like my flirting with her in the style of, well, the depression years?"

"You're too lazy for even that."

"In spite of his successful Egyptian campaign, Napoleon knew he couldn't take the fortress of Akkon."

An added presence. Rhetorical with embarrassment. Wrong to expect it would be a catalyst and help her with yellow fever, rainy blues and black ice. As unable as ever to break through Ada's reserve. Tied up in desires, surprising, half-admitted, knots twisted over and over, the twine too strong, too new. What if silence was already an answer? The moon unusually large and near. At times the sea rises into the light and becomes incomprehensible. Did she only imagine a new stiffness in Ada's shoulders? Discrepancies in latitudes? Did her eyes come to rest miles behind Amy's from habit, or fearing too intimate, too demanding?

Too difficult. If the voice continued to throw Alexander von Humboldt's shadow over his microscope while Columbus heads south for the gold, while the Creoles want a share in the government, while Hidalgo's revolutionary army begins its zigzag march on Mexico City, it would slow the dissolves. She would wander again in the garden where Montezuma's biceps shortens and bulges as he lifts his hand in greeting, where she must walk so slowly she could circle the house for every single lifting of the knee, her toe on the curve of the earth must form a straight line with her shinbone. Only then may she lower her henceforward. But the voice has stopped. The foot hovers above the shoe. Her thoughts turn on their own axis without finding an end or edge. Ada's eyes twinkle with turmoil in the atmosphere, currents and strata of different temperatures.

"My slob of a son," she said, "doesn't seem to take job hunting very seriously. He hasn't been out of the house in three days."

"He would say: like Beethoven, I work very slowly." Amy was happy. The chore of the *Poetic Terms* was turning to chuckles and charlotte russe. Ada was helping. "There are no jobs."

Ada had one leg propped on the chair. "He hasn't changed since he was two years old: eats and sleeps, eats and sleeps. And you encourage him."

Amy reached for the encyclopedia to check a date, check her stare. "Well, with a bird like you at dinner. It's like being on the scales all the time. And he's still here when you dwindle into remoteness."

A draft swept a sheaf of papers to the floor.

"Damn," said Ada with unusual vehemence, "that damn latch again. Now they're out of order." Started for the window and stopped, suddenly attentive, till the cat gave up chasing his tail.

"He doesn't even do his share of the house work. He counts on my being embarrassed enough to take them over."

"Don't."

Ada slammed the pages down. "You are as thick-skinned as he is."

Started to speak, hoist the flag, and stopped short. Not the moment. Heat, but in excess, of the wrong sort. Too much ballast to abolish slavery and launch full speed into the water. No ropes in case of need. Another meaning of elegy.

She is grateful for the blind. Light has always been her enemy, casting a huge, distressing shadow at her feet. A shadow even larger than her body, which absorbs her smaller gestures and gives back what it can: extravagance, exaggeration. An alternate, bleary body waiting to be assumed, if she only knew how, as by an angel. A little girl in the half-open door. Or Montezuma distraught and bewildered. He did not know what would happen.

And saw Ada move down the stairs, as if pulled, her shadow in the shaft of light, Paul's shadow in his door.

"Don't worry," she whispered to him, "Ada sees with her feet. But these nights can last years."

"I was on my way to the fridge," he admitted. "Even young Napoleon skipped class to sneak eggs and milk from Mère Marguérite. Later he preferred Château Lafite. Why don't we all snack, drink, pretend we know each other, have a party, get married?"

Stalked Ada who was leaning her cheek against the window, her right arm cradling her head. The parrots fly to the top of the trees where no one can see them. Paul touched his palm to her other cheek, as he must have done as a child, begging her to admit the touch of skin, the support of a chair, a glass of wine.

Ada's lids trembled as if ruffled by a breeze. The cat came up and rubbed against her. "Your father," she said after a while, "had a thing about muscles. The leg muscles in particular. He liked to sit and finger my calves."

Muffled sounds, incomprehensible, from all directions. A rolling, a rattle, a crack across the American voice. *Terracaliente,* she makes out, *adios* and *tiempodelagarua.* They are not words because she has no meaning for them, instead, glistening objects in the middle of a page, jewels on Cortés' velvet cloak, adding incalculable weight in the heat. Or else buzzing insects, covering Alexander von Humboldt's body till no part of it feels altogether comfortable, getting inside his clothes, their sting causing swellings which last for several weeks.

"Do you miss the stage?" it had occurred to her to ask Ada who was again watching the cat.

"It's amazing how he can keep it up," Ada pointed at the cat, "or a dervish."

It made Amy dizzy, "like going up in a balloon or climbing a mountain. Just looking at it, I have trouble breathing, my eyes must be getting bloodshot. But *your* eyes are in your feet. Distributed equally over their entire surface, if you like. That's why you have no sense of time or distance, delve into disappearance, a surface of hard work beyond all solids."

Stolid light. White, such a white wind, Victoria, the whirl, took both of Amy's hands that first time, as if she needed a rudder to navigate the eddies of her own words. Eyes unnaturally bright, she had thought, was it a sign of fever or of being Mexican? and looked around the room for rescue, a joke, a drink.

It was raining hard when they drove home. Watched the windshield wipers go back and forth, Ada's foot on the pedal, her black heel, her hands on the steering wheel.

"This trip to Mexico sounds attractive," she said, "I'd like to stretch my legs, let out a few seams, you know, thread the needle, get new ideas in the old head. God knows I could stand it. I've been looking at Tremont, Boylston, Pinckney so long I don't even see them any more. Time to change the movie."

"There are omens."

"OK, pull my leg. Don't you think it would be exciting to see a country so different? Like a dream playing on the outside, deserts with cactuses, burros dying of thirst in the implacable sun?"

"If that's what you want, the *National Geographic* should do nicely," Ada said a bit drily.

"That would not be in the spirit of adventure," she replied. "And this was a red light you just went through."

"The spirit of adventure is quite used to getting along without you."

"One would think you don't like the idea of this trip," she tried hard not to sound pleased. Was Ada jealous? A crack in her shell?

Alexander von Humboldt's main contribution to geology was his attentive study of the volcanoes of the New World. In spite of the distance, way up on the treacherous ice of Mt. Chimborazo, she can see blood oozing from his gums and lips. His eyes are red and blood-shot against the perpetual snow. Every breath is attended with sharp pains in the head and chest, the sharpening of doubt. He pauses, braced against the brush of the wind and fear of falling, looks up, beyond the peak, into the glacial light: What does my body want? Whereas in his personal life, the voice continues, his inner turmoil and frustration were carefully kept from erupting. We only have one single letter in which . . .

Such volumes of smoke, sparks and cinders were belched forth from its burning entrails and driven down the sides of the mountain as nearly suffocated Cortés' men. Sulfur was precipitated on the slopes of the crater. Volumes piled on her table, still all she knows of Mexico. The education of Aztec women. Nothing but dance and music. Hence they walked "as if carried by a cool wind," feeling their genitals with every step, with each swing of the arms, walked as if every move gave birth. Not like her hesitations which take back her steps before they can even take shape, bare intervals, itchy, hitched-up skirt. But perhaps she worried too much? Why not a coke instead, or coffee.

Ada showed no interest. She was typing.

"How about this for your travel brochure," said Paul: "Montezuma had the magicians locked up in the Cuauhcalco prison and their wives and children killed. The chiefs killed the women by hanging them with ropes, and the children by dashing them to pieces against the walls."

"Even violence," she said, "to jolt me out of my rut."

There was a pause in the typing. Ada bent over the sheet, inserting the correcting paper.

Paul continued: "The body of the sacrificed captive was delivered to the warrior who had taken him in battle, and by him, after being dressed, was served up in an entertainment to his friends. This was not the coarse repast of famished cannibals, but a banquet teeming with delicious beverages and delicate viands, prepared with art, and attended by both sexes. At another feast, the dedication of the great temple of Huitzilopochtli, prisoners who for some years had been reserved for the purpose, were drawn from all quarters to the capital. They were ranged in files, forming a procession nearly two miles long."

"Not just prisoners," she added. "Foreign tongues are not fit food for the Gods. The most beautiful of their own young men and women, the most accomplished dancers, the most intrepid young warriors were annually sacrificed. Nice to know I wouldn't have made the grade. You not either, Paul. Ada, however ... Maybe that's why she has an aversion to that country."

Ada was still typing when Victoria appeared.

"You," she turned to Ada, "must be Amy's companion. How I envy you. You will help me persuade her to come? Perhaps you come too?"

"I don't think Amy needs persuading," said Ada. "She is already studying the conquest of Mexico. So is my son, Paul."

"Would you like a sample?" said Paul, shaking hands. "In 1519, Patlahuatzin touched his hands to the ground and to his forehead in greeting. A few minutes later the Cholultecas had flayed his arms to the elbows and cut his hands at the wrists so that they dangled."

"How wonderful," said Victoria, taking her hand back. "I mean, that you are so thorough."

"Easier than leading a strenuous dream life," was all Amy could think.

"You'll get sick," said Ada. "I know you'll get sick as soon as the wind starts pushing at your plane."

The involuntary muscles in her viscera no longer go into spasms. She feels safer now and tired. She thinks of the stuccoed fruit on the ceiling. But her safety is hollow, a crowd of figures pressing in. Josephine Bonaparte smiles, skillfully hiding her bad teeth, Henry sniggers, and Beethoven wants his socks mended. She swallows centuries, continents, armies, wave after wave, Columbus, Cortés, Humboldt, their desire beating against the coast of America rising up inside her, incomprehensible. Don't drown me, they say, I want you. I want you because you are unlike me. Or did they say: like me? Boats setting out, day after day, for different waves, different shore lines in the distance, different air and sun. Or the same wave, the same air and sun, an island named Reinhard von Haeften, its interior unpenetrated, unexplored. She finds it nearly consoling to think of Humboldt training his telescope toward the blue officer's coat across the ocean. But returning from the distance, a little giddy still, he records with precision what he measured against the impossible blue: movement of planets, intensity of magnetic force, atmospheric disturbances, volcanoes in rows indicating vast subterranean fissures.

Paul was chilly and complained. "How long before the floors will be iced over and I'll have to skate to the phone to cut this ear-splitting ring."

The house was cold, the call not for him. He refused extra sweaters.

"Too many layers would cancel my features which are already blurred by bulk. For instance just now, taking Coleman off the turntable, the cold sharpening my bones, I had a sudden intimation of my true character without spelling lessons: I'll always stay a child skipping now on this foot and now on the other—because of the cold, you know—all through Massachusetts and the astonished neighboring states."

"You change your stance as fast as the record," she stole a look at Ada who was practicing her dervish whirl in the hall, round and round, and didn't seem to have noticed that the music had stopped and changed. "I suppose that has its excitement, like a ferris wheel or, rather, getting lost in the back yard, since the point seems to be surprise."

He stood beside her now, watching Ada. She was turning counter clockwise, as you must do in the northern hemisphere to be in accordance with the rotation of the earth.

"A vast twilight zone, nearly 1500 miles wide, is slipping around the earth," he said, "and if you get close it wheels you three subway stops past sanity and won't let you get off for dinner."

"You've never missed one. So all is not lost."

"You underestimate," he sulked. "My depression, like Beethoven's, is terrible and complete."

Alexander von Humboldt describes the Universe: a synthesis, bringing together, the danger of getting lost in the mountains of detail he keeps accumulating, oh, so patiently. The importance of connecting it all into a cosmos which opens out like the splendid white flower from the red disk of that fall-blooming annual.

Metaphor, she mumbles. Half my life I've spent connecting perceptions this way, by analogy. But the flower I'd have skipped. Only a scientist can afford such hackneyed comparisons.

She accepts, though, that without our connecting them into a picture the dots are not even visible, that being real means having form. Metaphor, muscles, telescopes, travelers. Columbus, the first to connect with the NEW WORLD: and the two hemispheres which God had cast asunder were united, how sexual, and began to become alike. Could Ada and she ever, could she wish it on her? This edge on her desire, leaning into aggression, violent games to play with Freud and sleepiness, like a relentless wind to continue the conversation.

Was Ada getting thinner? Was her silence a flutter or wary of thin ice between the lines of talk, loaded dice? Fits of cleaning. A sudden compulsion to wash windows, wipe the ribs of the radiators, why not let them stay dirty? An impression that she wanted to make a speech, utter warnings, or at least cough at regular intervals. Yet eluded questions. Faulty reading of stars, a level look at the backs of books. At least Amy had removed her childhood photo, the desperate, fat girl pushing out of her clothes. The quadrant decalibrated, a silk doublet and 10,000 maravedis to him who should first see land. Follow the great flocks of birds which scatter, musicians tuning up, notes that do not lead into, disconnected, mosquito bites on Amy's skin, impossible in Boston, in mid-December, but an edgy feel of discomfort. She looked into the mirror to see if her skin was flaking off, saw the usual wrinkles and the back of Ada's left shoulder slipping into her coat, then getting covered by a silk scarf which she wore on top in the French manner, then moving out of the field.

She must be getting well. She can concentrate much better. A short time ago her head went so fast down the freeway. Its interior still has a population unmatched by other environments: dancers walking as if carried by a cool wind, Cortés takes off his helmet, the Creoles demand participation in the government, an eruption of the Chimborazo, the fleet proceeds with a strong breeze until sunset, the procession slowly mounts the temple steps up to the *piedra di sacrificios,* led by the Empress Josephine, waves crash through the wall. But now, if she thinks of Ada, she can hold still long enough to ask herself if this is the same figure as the dancing mistress of her dream. And when the whirl starts up again, it is not Ada who begins to move away, but something on the periphery: insurgents on the run as the viceregal forces take the offensive, an Acapulco louse scurrying away from Alexander von Humboldt's microscope.

It always begins on the south side of the room which, being nearer the equator, travels the faster. So that Napoleon's army advancing into the *terra fria* actually marches in circles and is easily captured by Montezuma's men in their feather armor. Napoleon sticks his hand into his coat. Whether or not the gesture is of an amatory nature, the offense is capital. The tribunal pronounces unity in diversity. Alexander von Humboldt listens in profound silence. Tears stream down his face.

Ada stared at the dripping, watched each drop round itself, hang in precarious perfection, then give in to excess, oblong, and fall. The taps didn't quite close any more. But she listened as if trying to trap what? The point between stillness and motion? The birth of gravity? Degrees of tension and attention? Then she pushed her hair back with the fluttering motion of her arm and turned again, slowly, round and round, counter-clockwise, like water swirling, turns and more turns.

We do not often think of the movement of the earth which seems so solid and immovable, we simply submit to the succession of night and day. Only in her sleep can Amy feel its astonishing speed whirling her relentlessly eastward, undoing all research and exploration toward the west. Nothing will bite the bait of words here, no fishing between the lines though hundreds of girls are taking off their clothes. As long as it is only the rotation of the earth's axis, she can still hold on with hands and knees as in a strong wind. But if she suddenly experiences the other, much faster movement around the sun, then she is truly lost, bits of naked flesh spinning off into vast spaces, swallowed whole and instantly forgotten, at best caught in the large twilight zone that slips continually around the globe and abolishes all outsides.

Had she pushed too hard when she spoke again to Ada of her restlessness, her sudden desire to roam, a strange country, strange cities, a language she didn't know. She thought it would sound like bunches of spring, field flowers in the ear. No way of seeing dry cracks in the sentences.

Had Ada felt pushed on stage in a part she hadn't rehearsed? "Go to your bloody Mexico. But do you have to be at me? Do I have to like it too?"

Amy felt the blow to her head. Sat there, stunned.

"I'm sorry, I didn't mean to hit you," Paul came from the dining room, "I just thought I'd create a diversion."

Ada's face above hers, forehead beaded with sweat. "Are you hurt? Let me get you a compress." Left the room with a sureness in her bearing that comes out of having answered a difficult question.

Amy bent down and picked up *The Conquest of Mexico.*

She opens her eyes again to the reassuring square of the shade, its outlines dimmer, reddish, pretending to be straight lines, to coordinate her field of vision, but green now. Strange, this moving in and out of the spin, as if it were a matter of breathing, a constant chemical transformation of vertigo into vertical, the deceptive solidity of lungs.

Walked slowly toward the Common, making her way as through dense underbrush. Thick clouds between the roofs. The air cold and hard as marble. Beyond, in the trees, the souls of ancestors. If only Ada had thrown the book. It would have meant punctuation, a new departure, crossing oceans, visiting castles, train rides, watching bullfights even, and writing postcards back to Paul. But Paul, just one more silliness, like the silly swan boats she used to watch here in summer, and the ducks. But now scum had dried to a greyish brown which covered the bottom and the stones around the edge, stones which had looked polished, like duck eggs.

With effort she unstuck her sole. Slow afternoon. In spite of the season, the drained lake, the brown squalor of the dry lawn, the narrow sun, there were people. Brushed against sullen teenagers horsing around, eyes full of watery sky-grey, old men, purposeful women with shopping bags. Slow afternoon. So hard to understand. Ada, she thought, how she draws me and keeps just, just barely out of my reach. Why would her nails keep growing after her death, after their world had slipped away? Pushed her face upward into the fine drizzle.

She would go to Mexico. Not just for the translations and readings. In the harsher light, the space between them would have to change, the landscape come out of the fog, forced into definition.

Now the light around the shade has grown so pale she wonders it if is there at all, if her eyes are not simply projecting this faint frame, a thin line to stop her eyes, a momentary *terra firma* the color of sleep or a silk doublet.

Desires, the voice says, to look at the stars, to climb a mountain, to describe the universe. The ocean bulges between them and the pain has been dulled to the point of disappearing. Life seems exciting and full of other caves to be explored. Not many of them, it is true, will yield an unknown species like the *guacharo* or oil bird with its enormous wingspan and edible fat between its legs, but all promise encounters beyond the tickle of fear, hoarse bird cries and clanging as of castanets.

Amy wades through the birdlime, next to Alexander von Humboldt. With effort, they unstick their soles, lift their knees and again let their feet touch the viscous mass with their toes. They duck to avoid the stalactites. She would like to discover a garden here, in this cave. But the prosody allows no liberties, the plants that spring up in this subterranean dark are pale and ghostly, deformed varieties without scent, and the Indians cannot be persuaded to go any farther.

The room has become invisible. It is only through her body touching the sheets, cool, clean, constantly changed, that she can hold on to her body as it sinks under its own weight into shadows that exceed comprehension. Here, birds are singing. Birds flutter from tree to tree as if drunk on air. Or is it the dancing mistress, slim as a thread, the way she stretches, the way she seems to breathe with her arms, her hair like ruffled feathers. Her slightest move as if carried by a cool wind. And over it all the ceiling with its stuccoed fruit. Why did they never fall?

"Mere contact with the free air," says Alexander von Humboldt indifferently, "exercises a soothing influence on the wary spirit and calms the storm of passions." He is lying in a hammock, scratching with his left hand, while the telescope in his right is trained on a black surface of glazed volcanic sand and lava, the fragments of which, its boiling arrested in fantastic forms, impede the advance of Cortés' men.

"They too are going in circles," says Amy, as smoke, sparks and cinders belch forth from the crater. "They too will be captured by time."

"I'll show you the cosmos," says Alexander von Humboldt and draws lines isodynamic, isoclinal, isothermal stretching between all the petals of the fall-blooming annual, then follows them hand in hand with Amy. If only Napoleon were not invading her body. They walk on the surface heavy with grief where the height of the barometer reduced to sea level is always the same. Here the rock beds have the same dip and the magnetic needle the same inclination to the plumb line. Alexander von Humboldt's head is a ring composed of atoms of only one element relating to zones of force, having equal angles, equal tension, equal value, all edges equally foreshortened.

Love, she said, into the rain, and pictured Ada showing a student how to keep her heel turned out while her foot glides forward without lifting the toe from the floor. The two bodies moved in parallel with the teasing lag of imitation, like two waves following one another with the same diminishing speed. The gilded roof of the State House glistening in the drizzle. The dancers' faces empty inside their frames of feathery hair. Unknown species. A wingspan of 1.13 meters. The rain was against Ada. Or Amy's desire?

Amy opens her eyes. Though it is dark and she can see absolutely nothing, it makes a great difference to her movement. For a moment she thinks she has reached the polar regions. Everything is much slower, if not standing still. Her body is so vast now, nothing can surprise her. But as her lids go shut again, a flock of birds, is it geese? parrots? lifts off, beating the air with a thunder of cries, and here is again the ceiling under which childhood waits to be left behind. This is why she must learn to walk on her hands. Two older girls take hold of her legs. Her hair is hanging down to the floor, her skirt falls over her belt down over her neck. Thus, legs high in the air, she walks across the stone floor, a moving island surfacing from the music that has spread all over the ground. Again and again, till the teachers turn away: "Her thighs are too fat," she hears, "and she already has pubic hair."

Found Ada in the study, reading the passage where the sacrificial procession moved through the orderly streets, girls in long white gowns seeming to glide above the ground. Crowds of people were cheering, showering them with flowers. A procession of boys, also in white gowns, approached from the other side as they mounted the temple steps toward the priest in the white robe, toward the great black stone, toward the flaming sun. Again tried to measure the degree of feeling admitted.

"Is it so different?" Ada's eyes focused some distance behind Amy. "Music and dance was the bulk of my schooling also. The body. I remember all-day lessons about the hips. The hips as the center from which all walking was willed and directed. We must not feel the ground under our feet, we must not feel our feet. The hips, only the hips. We must think with the hips. And as for being prepared for sacrifice . . ."

"How you exaggerate," she said instead of: you know I couldn't bear not to see you tilting your head in this way you have, or your eyes focusing just a little behind me. She would say it some other time. Your walk, she would say, as if you were pulled. And sexual. Fusing with space and giving birth to movement. Or at tea, at table and voices mingle, hovering in the morning when first stretching your mind into the fissures of air.

She would like to hear more of Alexander von Humboldt's physical description of the universe, of connecting the million details, of bringing together, activity shared by muscle and mind, by explorer, scientist, poet, mechanic. She wants to ask him about sex, straight out, connecting body with body.

"I am not hungry," he replies, walking away. "The icy pole or point of the greatest cold no more corresponds with the terrestrial pole than the word promise. Aberration is by no means confined to the sun."

She can no longer hear him now, though she still sees his figure in the distance, waving his arms and slapping his body. The only effective defense against insects, he has told her earlier.

Why is she unable to hold all that is happening to her? Parts of her body are orbiting now around her head, or is it another sun, her thoughts scattering into the atmosphere. She would like to partition them all off in order to study them with distance, with objectivity, lined up on a sheet of paper large enough to encompass the revolving elements and, as under a magnifying glass, she sees pores or, rather, specks of dust in the snow crystals packed tight. She walks across on her hands.

Birds have to eat all the time, somebody says, but now she is bored, she has heard it before.

II

A Form of Memory

Physical Description of Motion

Alexander von Humboldt shipped out on the mail boat "Pizarro" with sextants, quadrants, scales, compasses, telescopes, microscopes, hygrometer, barometer, eudimeter, thermometer, chronometer, magnetometer, a Leiden bottle, *lunettes d'épreuves* and a botanist, Aimé Bonpland.

Before him, using the newly improved astrolabe to determine the ship's position, Columbus had thrown his coin not as a mere adventurer, but with a plan.

The mistress drew the switch through her left hand and smiled at each of us in turn.

"Stress" is used for metrical stress whereas "accent" is reserved for the emphasis demanded by language.

The mistress showed us how to walk, hitching up her skirts so that we could see her legs far above the knees.

All landmarks disappeared, and the sea horizon extended all the way round the sky.

A bad omen. Like a flaming ear of corn in the sky, bleeding fire, drop by drop. Like a wound in the sky. The magicians told Montezuma that what was to come would come swiftly.

Even before Columbus, the earth turned on its axis to divide the day from night and afford a convenient means of measuring time.

Alexander von Humboldt knew that Columbus' inspiration "from the heart" had been a flock of parrots flying toward the southwest, a word with level stress where the accent falls with equal emphasis on both syllables. Birds, said Alexander von Humboldt. All land is discovered by birds. He lifted his field glasses, but could see nothing but an expanse of water apparently boundless.

The mistress slightly lifted a knee and let her foot touch the ground with the tip of her toes which formed a straight line with the shinbone. Only then did she slowly lower her heel. Her full, round, delicate knee stretched at the moment the heel came down.

In spite of the successful Egyptian campaign, Napoleon could not take the fortress of Akkon or reduce the bulge of the equatorial regions.

Alexander von Humboldt talked twice as fast as Napoleon, and in mixed German, French, Spanish and English. He reserved Hebrew for intimate letters. No wonder there were rumors. (See Henriette Herz.)

Montezuma had the magicians locked up in the Cuauhcalco prison and their wives and children killed. The chiefs killed the women by hanging them with ropes, and the children by dashing them to pieces against the walls.

Reference

Humboldt, Alexander, Baron von (1769–1859), German naturalist and scientific explorer.

Physical Description of Motion, Continued

The action of a muscle is to contract, or shorten in length, and thus the two structures to which it is attached are brought closer together.

We had to hitch up our skirts to the hips and walk so slowly that I could have run around the whole house for every single step. If we put down a foot too quickly the mistress' switch was on our calves.

Enter Beethoven: I shall take fate by the throat.

Alexander von Humboldt had fallen in love with a young officer, Reinhard von Haeften, notwithstanding the rumors about Henriette Herz.

Metaphor implies a relationship between two terms which are thus brought together in the muscle.

The hips were the center from which all walking was willed and directed. We must not feel the ground under our feet. We must not feel our feet. We must feel nothing but our hips. We must think with our hips.

As Alexander von Humboldt's boat approached the Antilles typhoid immobilized most of the passengers. The Spanish flag moved up and down the mast.

Montezuma received the messengers in the House of the Serpent and ordered two captives to be painted with chalk. Like metaphor, this required an eye for resemblance and clear skies. The two captives were then sacrificed before the messengers' eyes: their breasts torn open, and the messengers sprinkled with their blood. This was done because the messengers had seen the gods.

Reference

1799–1804, Alexander von Humboldt and Aimé Bonpland undertook their famous expedition to South America which led them to Teneriffe, Venezuela (the Orinoco-Casiquiare region), Colombia, Ecuador (ascent of Mt. Chimborazo up to 5760 m) and Mexico.

Illustration

Alexander von Humboldt wears a yellow coat. Yellow is the color of envy, fever, and the hair of Reinhard von Haeften's fiancee.

The sky and mountains in the distance are blue and match Alexander von Humboldt's pants. Aimé Bonpland wears black the better to merge into the background. He is confident that his coat will not absorb enough light quanta to hinder his examination of an orchid.

The natives, painted toward the upper right, wear loincloths to cover their *verguenzas* or "shames." The magnitude of these areas exercises a powerful influence on the quantity of humidity contained in the atmosphere.

Connections

When Columbus set foot on the new world, the two hemispheres which God had cast asunder were reunited and began to become alike.

La Malinche translated the Nahuatl of the messengers into Mayan for Jeronimo de Aguilar, who then translated it into Spanish for the conquistadors.

Our running had to be as if we were carried by a cool wind. Our heels were not to touch the ground. This was to give us beautiful legs.

Montezuma sent captives to the Spaniards because they might be gods and wish to drink blood.

It was not the tidal wave that advanced westerly, only its form.

From Kosmos or Physical Description of the Universe

There is, perhaps, some truth in the accusation advanced against many German scientific works, that they lessen the value of their investigations by an accumulation of detail and do not sufficiently connect the latter into general laws. (See muscle.)

Eyewitness Report

Cortés took off his helmet and stroked his beard.

A vast twilight zone, nearly 1500 miles wide, was slipping around the earth as the latter turned on its axis.

Aimé Bonpland sat under a tree. His hands were resting a book on his knees. He was memorizing Linnaeus' *Species Plantarum.*

The Creoles aspired to a larger participation in the government, whereas the incumbent viceroy hoped that patriotism would supersede the desire for social reform.

The Aztec harlots bathed frequently, a heathenish idiosyncracy to Father Sahagún.

No part of Alexander von Humboldt's body felt altogether comfortable. His face and neck were burned. The skin was flaking off. He was unable to shave. Every exposed part of his body was bitten by insects. Some had even found their way inside his clothes.

A small river ran through the middle of the garden, and on the banks hundreds of girls were taking off their clothes. We swam as far as the sluice gate which joins the park wall. When we dressed again, the whole river was already in the shade and a fine mist rising from the ground.

Priests introduced *Paradise Lost.*

Volcanoes

Alexander von Humboldt was seized by a sudden desire to climb the Teneriffe. Increasing cold seeped through his light tropical clothing even though the steep mountain side caught the rays of the sun at a less oblique angle. Alexander von Humboldt paused to examine the stones and catch his breath. Sulphurous fumes burned holes into his jacket, and his hands got stiff at 2° Celsius.

Eyewitness Report, Continued

After the alexandrine had become the accepted meter for French tragedy, four viceroys came and went in rapid succession.

The Empress Josephine skillfully hid her bad teeth.

Gravitation, Bonpland explained to her, elongates the watery envelope of the earth very slightly in two opposite directions.

Elegy

The term elegy was at one time applied to work on any subject, composed in the elegiac meter.

When Alexander von Humboldt returned to Europe on August 1, 1804, he learned that the French and German newspapers had regretfully announced his death, by yellow fever, in Acapulco.

Years earlier, Montezuma's eldest son had entered into a poetical correspondence with one of his father's concubines, a woman who wrote verses with ease and discussed matters of state with the king and his ministers.

The only ugly people I had ever seen were the two old women who cooked and cleaned. Their faces were like bark. The thought that they might take off their clothes made me gag.

A later meaning of elegy was a poem in whatever meter in which a twilight zone slips around the globe.

Whether or not the correspondence was of an amorous nature, the offense was capital. The tribunal pronounced sentence of death on the unfortunate prince, and the king, steeling his heart against all entreaties and the voice of nature, suffered the cruel judgment to be carried into execution. Then he shut himself up in his palace for many weeks and had the doors and windows of his son's residence walled up, so that it might never again be occupied.

Exercise

The foot should not rest on the big toe, but the weight of the body should be distributed equally over the entire surface of the foot.

Elegy, Continued

The two ecclesiastics recited the Lord's prayer to the idolatrous Indians. The natives listened in profound silence. Tears streamed down their cheeks.

The Empress Josephine declared to the assembled court that, no longer having any hope of bearing children who could satisfy the Emperor's political needs and the interest of France, she, with the permission of her august spouse, was pleased to give him a divorce.

The viceregal forces took the offensive. The insurgents were soon captured and executed. Their heads were hung in cages at the four corners of the city.

As a considerable portion of the qualitative properties of matter is still unknown to man, the attempt to describe the universe must prove unsuccessful. Thus, there lurked in Alexander von Humboldt's mind an unsatisfied longing, tinged with sadness.

Physical Description of Motion, Continued

The Indians had never entered the cave of the *guacharos,* or "oil birds," farther than the first chamber. Beyond, in the dark, lived the souls of ancestors along with the birds.

Alexander von Humboldt insisted on wading on through the bird-lime and the biting smoke of their torches. With effort he unstuck his sole, lifted his knee and let his foot touch the viscous mass with his toe. He did not always lower his heel, but simply straightened his knee and lifted the other foot.

Three girls and three boys we were in our room and shy with one another. One night, the mistress pulled my covers off and carried me naked out of the house. In the garden, she put me into a small box which exactly fitted my size, and closed the lid.

Alexander von Humboldt found strange formations of subterranean plants which grew, pale and ghostly, in the dark cave. The Indians looked at the deformed plants with fear and could not be persuaded to penetrate any farther into the cave.

Napoleon asked: "What is the matter?"

The prosody allowed for liberties, but Alexander von Humboldt ducked to avoid the stalactites.

Now and then, when one of the Indian guides raised his torch, Alexander von Humboldt and Aimé Bonpland could get a glimpse of a momentarily blinded bird. They fired into the dark vault, in the direction of the loudest screams.

I remember nothing further until I saw daylight come through the holes in my box. Then my little coffin was put upright and opened. I felt dizzy as I stepped out into the light.

The two specimens Aimé Bonpland killed proved the guacharo to be indeed an unknown species. It was the size of a crow, with a wingspan of 1.13 meters and an enormous beak. Between their legs the young birds had a thick lump of edible fat.

"What a battlefield this would make," said Napoleon.

Reference

Bonpland, Aimé (1773–1858), French botanist and Alexander von Humboldt's companion on their famous expedition to South America (1799–1804).

Physical Description of Sexual Intercourse

The explorer travels over the beloved body, but nowhere does he find an end or edge.

When Columbus set foot on the Bahamas, the two worlds which God had cast asunder were reunited and began to become alike.

The laying on of a gold ring cures excessive lucidity.

The moon unusually large and near. At times, the sea rises into the light and becomes incomprehensible.

The contract is definite when the man steps into the woman's shoe. As long as the foot still hovers above the shoe, his body may still turn on its own axis, which takes about twenty-four hours.

Reference

Haeften, Reinhard von (1773-?)

Volcanoes, Continued

Alexander von Humboldt was seized by a sudden desire to climb a volcano, mountain or at least staircase.

Toward autumn I got into strange states at night. I would be awakened by a deafening noise, a roar and thundering. The first few times I screamed out loud. The other girls jumped out of their beds and then got angry when all they could hear was the splash of the fountain in the courtyard. Xada would sit with me till I calmed down. But as soon as I put my head on the pillow I heard thunder and storms or wild music, loud as if my ear were the soundboard.

Three years later, representatives of aspiring emancipators in both New Spain and New Granada arrived in London to solicit arms and munitions in exchange for discrepancies of longitude.

Beethoven's overbearing manners were not those of an uncouth provincial misbehaving himself in all innocence.

The track opened onto a black surface of glazed volcanic sand and lava, the broken fragments of which, arrested in its boiling progress in a thousand fantastic forms, opposed continual impediments to Cortés' advance. Amidst these, one huge rock, the *Pico del Fraile,* rose to the perpendicular height of 160 feet, compelling the conquistadors to take a wide circuit. They soon came to the limits of perpetual snow where new difficulties presented themselves, as the treacherous ice gave imperfect footing, and a false step might precipitate them into the frozen chasms that yawned around. To increase their distress, respiration in these aerial regions became so difficult, that every effort was attended with sharp pains in the head and limbs. Still they pressed on, till, drawing nearer the crater, such volumes of smoke, sparks and cinders were belched forth from its burning entrails, and driven down the sides of the mountain, as nearly suffocated and blinded them. Sulphur was precipitated on the sides of the crater.

Footnote

If the object is to obtain sulphur for gunpowder, it is on the whole less inconvenient to import it from Spain.

Physical Description of Sexual Intercourse, Continued

"Aimé," said Alexander von Humboldt.
Aimé Bonpland recited the *Species Plantarum* by Linnaeus.

Etiquette

Knowing that the alexandrine takes its name from the Old French romance on Alexander the Great, Alexander von Humboldt learned to dance the samba, the animalito and the congo-minuet.

The mistress always smiled as she switched us.

The body of the sacrificed captive was delivered to the warrior who had taken him in battle, and by him, after being dressed, was served up in an entertainment to his friends. This was not the coarse repast of famished cannibals, but a banquet teeming with delicious beverages and delicate viands, prepared with art, and attended by both sexes. At another feast, the dedication of the great temple of Huitzilopochtli, in 1486, prisoners who for some years had been reserved for the purpose, were drawn from all quarters to the capital. They were ranged in files, forming a procession nearly two miles long.

Exercise

The right foot glides forward, without lifting the toe from the floor. The heel is kept as much turned out as possible, which makes it feel as if the movement were begun by the heel.

Reference

Humboldt's services to geology were mainly based on his attentive study of the volcanoes of the New World. He showed that they fell into linear groups, presumably corresponding with vast subterranean fissures.

Physical Description of Alexander von Humboldt as Kosmos-Machine

1) The Platform:
   the tropics, painted in oil, very blue, the distant mountains, palm trees and, under the microscope, cactus, orchids, parrots, maps and oilbirds

2) The Scaffolding:
   a) yellow coat
   b) gold buttons
   c) striped shirt
   d) blue-striped trousers
   e) worn straw hat
   f) Wellington boots

3) The Circuits:
   gathering, measuring, sorting, classifying, coding, comparing, filing, abstracting, connecting, connecting, connecting

4) The Knife:
   had loved young men, Reinhard von Haeften, Bougainville's son, age 15, not Aimé Bonpland who is off with a native woman, spends nights writing

5) The Basket:
   Scattered Remarks on Basalt
   On the Original Inhabitants of America and the Monuments They Left behind
   Memoir on Sea Currents
   Political Essay on the Kingdom of New Spain
   Essay on the Geography of Plants
   Views of the Cordilleras

Critical Examination of the Discovery of America
Historical Account of the Voyage to the Equinoctial Regions of the New Continent
Kosmos or Physical Description of the Universe

6) The Waste:
vain, famous, an excellent dancer, talkative in many languages

Elegy, Continued

At last they came. At last they began to march toward us. Their horses carried them on their backs wherever they wished. They came in battle array, as conquerors, and the dust rose in whirlwinds on the road.

I looked at the horse and saw my first teacher, Yamada. The position of the feet was her. The proud bearing was her, the fiery eyes and the way of shaking its mane. A girl held the reins. When she saw me stop and gape she clicked her tongue and led the horse in a circle. I ran alongside. The horse's rump was overwhelming, so huge, so inhuman. Frightening. And yet, the rump most of all reminded me of Yamada. The same calm movement, the same sure strength, and the way the thighs moved against each other. I suddenly felt faint.

No part of Alexander von Humboldt's body felt altogether comfortable. His face and neck were burned. The skin was flaking off. He was unable to shave. Every exposed part of his body was bitten by insects. Some had even found their way inside his clothes.

A line from which unstressed syllables have been dropped is called truncated.

Then the slaughter began: knife strokes and sword strokes and death. The people of Cholula had not foreseen it, had not suspected it. They faced the Spaniards without weapons, without their swords or their shields.

Alexander von Humboldt examined the Great Cholulan Pyramid with leisure and his usual care.

Even before his hearing deteriorated, Beethoven was downcast and distressed.

In 1519, Patlahuatzin touched his hands to the ground and to his forehead. A few minutes later the Cholultecas had flayed his arms to the elbows and cut his hands at the wrists so that they dangled.

Among the attempts to refer all that is unstable in the sensuous world to a single principle, the theory of gravitation is the most comprehensive and the richest in cosmic results.

Hypothesis

If the colonials had not vaccillated and fumbled, if Aloysio Galvani had first stimulated the nervous fiber by spherical form, if Pythagoras had thought the earth was an Aztec calendar, if Montezuma had explained the accidental contact of two heterogeneous metals

Poetry

Alexander von Humboldt wanted to write an epithalamium for Reinhard von Haeften's wedding.

His voluntary muscles included many parallel striated fibers, bound together by connective tissue. Their opposite ends were fastened to the separate bones by extensions of the connective tissue.

Alexander von Humboldt could not find any feminine rhymes. He returned to the study of volcanoes, arranging them in linear groups indicating vast subterranean fissures.

Physical Description of Motion, Continued

Alexander von Humboldt and Aimé Bonpland were walking back from the beach, peeling their soles off the ground, when Alexander von Humboldt sensed somebody behind them.

I shall never forget the entrance of Cempada, the new dancing mistress, as long as I live. The outline of her body was sharp against the light, her hair like ruffled feathers. Slim as a thread, the way she stretched, the way she seemed to breathe with her arms, the luxurious drop of her shoulders. Her every slightest movement showed the pleasure she took in her body.

Alexander von Humboldt, whose muscles had a density of 1.055, turned and saw a tall mestizo, almost naked, about to bring a club down on his head. He ducked, but Bonpland caught the blow on his temple.

For weeks I saw her before my eyes and nearly expected that her image would take on flesh. She wore a tight netting of blue glass pearls as a corsage which left her breasts bare, circling them with two rings of larger and darker pearls. I had never seen naked breasts and wondered if my chest would grow to look like hers.

The mestizo paid no more attention to Humboldt, but went to pick up Bonpland's hat which lay in the sand, a few feet off.

Her feet were bare.

Meanwhile Bonpland had come to, lunged at his aggressor and chased him into a thicket which, Alexander von Humboldt did not fail to notice, consisted mostly of torch thistles or *cactus cereus.*

I was most surprised when she lifted her arms and I saw dense tufts of black hair in her armpits.

Food

The incumbent viceroy hopes to profit by catering to the creoles.

The man from the Rio Negro declared that the meat of the manimodas monkey was only slightly inferior to human flesh.

I am not hungry, said Alexander von Humboldt.

Reference

Humboldt's inquiries into the origin of tropical storms afforded the earliest clue to the laws governing atmospheric disturbances.

Volcanoes, Continued

Comparing local times all the way round the globe, the Cabildos deposed the Spanish authorities and created provincial juntas.

Beethoven proposed marriage to Therese von Malfatti.

I am still not hungry, said Alexander von Humboldt.

At this moment, when the dance was loveliest, when song was linked to song and the meridians converged downward, the Spaniards killed the celebrants.

Eyewitness Report, Continued

The whole air reeked with smoke. The soldiers' faces were blackened with it. Some were using their ramrods, others putting powder on the touch-pans or taking charges from their pouches. Others again were firing into the smoke. A pleasant humming and whistling of bullets was heard. A soldier with a bleeding head and no cap was being dragged back by two men who supported him under the arms. Another was still standing, swinging his arm which had just been hurt while blood was streaming over his greatcoat as from a bottle.

Napoleon sat on his camp stool.

Montezuma bowed his head without speaking a word. For a long time he remained thus, with his head bent down. And when he spoke at last, it was only to say: What help is there now? Is there a mountain for us to climb?

Hypothesis

It is by subjecting isolated observations to the process of combination and comparison that we discover the climatic distribution of erections.

Rhyme, or repetition of the same or similar sounds, also serves to establish a connection between words and fear of flying (blue).

At sea, latitude is usually found by observing the altitude of some celestial body when crossing the meridian of the opposite sex.

Eyewitness Report, Continued

On the day Alexander von Humboldt climbed the Chimborazo, the atmospheric pressure sank as he got higher. He developed trouble breathing. Blood started to seep from his gums and lips. His eyes were red and blood-shot.

Columbus promised a silk doublet to the first man to see land.

Involuntary muscle could be found in the internal organs or viscera of Alexander von Humboldt's body, as in the walls of the digestive tract, blood vessels, respiratory passage and urinary and genital organs. It was capable of slow but protracted contractions.

Reference

After nine years as Josephine Bonaparte's gardener at Malmaison, Aimé Bonpland returned, in 1816, to South America where he was caught in a border quarrel between Argentina and Paraguay, and arrested by Dr. Francia's henchmen. Released after nine years' imprisonment, he settled in Borja, near the Brasilian border with an Indian wife and grew oranges peaches figs and roses. Though showered with medals and honorary diplomas, he never returned to Europe.

Alexander Von Humboldt's Dream

At daybreak, the Chimborazo showed a second peak, high above the first. Alexander von Humboldt was seized by the desire to climb both and thus explain the alternation of actuality and illusion by the rotation of the mind on its axis.

Hypothesis

Reinhard von Haeften

Volcanoes, Continued

While New Spain, like Venezuela, New Granada and Chile, was the scene of bloody combat, we must picture Beethoven in a turbulent emotional condition.

A volcano, properly so called, exists only where a permanent connection is established between the interior of the earth and the atmosphere, and the orgasm continues for long periods of time.

News from the mother country bent the motion of light rays out of their course which caused the Creoles to aspire to larger participation in the government.

When one of us said "I," she meant her body. Her body from head to toe. We felt ourselves more in our calves than in our eyes. I don't remember what anyone said. I remember how each girl walked.

This involves the action of muscle, which is to contract, or shorten in length. Thus the two structures to which it is attached are brought closer together.

The insurgents were unconcerned with the eccentricity of the earth's orbit. They desired immediate freedom from oppression.

Time

It is now clear that the turning of the earth on its axis is of very great service, not only to the astronomer, but to mankind in general, as affording a very convenient means of measuring time.

Volcanoes, Continued

A desperate conflict ensued, in which the patriots managed to avoid defeat until an ill-timed earthquake destroyed their morale. The settlements in control of the rebels were almost annihilated, while those remaining faithful to the king escaped unharmed. The clergy drew the expected conclusion.

Alexander von Humboldt was seized by a sudden desire to be a bird.

"Well," said Napoleon.

Nothing ever seemed to happen to us. All we did was dance and play music and grow, dance and play music and grow, dance and

Exercise (Les Ballets Russes)

Anna Pavlova forced Serge Lifar's knees wide open in a plié. His heels stayed on the floor until he could not stretch his tendons farther. Tamara Karsavina lowered and raised Nijinsky's arm, while Agrippina Vaganova pointed Serge Lifar's toes in a degagé, and Nijinsky relaxed Ida Rubinstein's instep. Galina Ulanova felt every muscle along Karsavina's back. Since Pavlova's battement penetrated into the very substance of the various ligaments of Michel Fokine's leg, Ida Rubinstein's heel remained turned out with the movement of Michel Fokine's toe so that Tamara Karsavina's leg was thrown through the first position forward to the angle of 90°, and Vera Trefilova's body bent backwards to repeat the same with somebody else's leg.

Physical Description of Sexual Intercourse, Continued

A virgin had best be offered to a passing stranger whose centrifugal force lessens his attraction everywhere except at the poles. If there are no strangers, the husband must wrap his finger in a white cloth which is torn into bloody bits and distributed to the priests. This does not cause pain to the husband.

On Friday afternoon, at 3:45, Beethoven requested that Frau Nanette Streicher mend his socks.

A refrain is not unusual.

Napoleon surveyed the locality with a profound air.

The interior remained unfamiliar to Alexander von Humboldt.

Interpolation

Columbus observed that the world was not round but pear-shaped, round except where it has a nipple.

Historical Moment

The leaders of the people were confused and divided.

Physical Description of Motion, Continued

In my new class I was made to walk on my hands. Two older girls took hold of my legs. My hair hung down to the floor, my skirt fell over the belt down over my neck. Thus, legs high in the air I walked across the stone floor.

In 1794, Antonio Narino had published a Spanish translation of the French Declaration of the Rights of Man. He was first imprisoned, then sent into exile.

Columbus sent out parties to the gold region of Cibao as soon as loss by radiation exceeded the daily quantity of heat received.

The simultaneous contraction of many fibers caused Montezuma's biceps to shorten and bulge, as he lifted his hand in greeting. Since his striated muscles were under conscious control this gesture was considered voluntary.

The women's shadows grew longer.

That same year the equinoxes traveled westward about fifty and one quarter inches.

Hidalgo began a zigzag advance toward the viceregal capital. Town after town, San Miguel, Celaya, Guanajuato, Guadalajara, Valladolid, fell at the onslaught of his ever increasing hordes. Near the end of October 1810, he encamped with an undisciplined multitude within eighteen miles of Mexico City. He might have taken the capital if he had pressed on.

Beethoven worked very slowly while the prime meridian passed through the Royal Observatory of Greenwich.

The delay proved fatal. It gave the commander of the viceregal forces time to assemble his troops and take the offensive. The insurgents and the royalists confronted each other on the banks of the Lerma river, forty miles from Guadalajara.

Explanation

Montezuma arrayed himself in his finery, preparing to go out and meet the Spaniards.

Physical Description of Motion, Continued

The royalists were all but defeated when an explosion set fire to a grass field occupied by the main body of Hidalgo's army. Stampeded by the smoken and flames, the rebels broke rank and fled.

From Kosmos or Physical Description of the Universe

While we consider volcanoes as intermittent springs emitting a fluid mixture of oxydized metals, alkalies and earths, we also remember with pleasure that Plato traced vaginal lubrication to eruptions of the Pyriphlegethon.

Figurative Language

That in which the literal meaning of words is disregarded in order to show diverse things as connected in a relationship, usually of resemblance. For instance: "Alexander von Humboldt did not care a fig," an expression derived from the ancient talisman in the shape of a clenched fist with the tip of the thumb emerging between the joints of the middle fingers. A symbolic representation of coitus. Alexander von Humboldt did not care for it.

Exercise

The leg is forcefully thrown forward, describing a circle backward on the height of 90° by rotating the hip joint.

Foot

See meter.

Physical Description of Sexual Intercourse, Continued

As the explorer approaches the beloved he recites a poem, preferably using frequent enjambment. The beloved prepares herself for the encounter by having the explorer's coat of arms tattooed on her belly. Ropes are to be kept near in case of need. The couple now throw off ballast, hoist the flag and launch full speed ahead into the water.

Variant

The beloved prepares himself for the encounter by having the explorer's coat of arms tattooed on his belly.

Repeat

Ropes are to be kept near in case of need.

Explanation

The insurgent colonies failed to wrest their independence from the force of gravity.

Alexander von Humboldt's muscle cells were cylindrical, scarcely 50μ in diameter, but some measured an inch or more in length. Each cell was surrounded by a delicate sarcolemma and contained several long nuclei.

The revolutionary armies were untrained, inexperienced, poorly equipped. No assistance was received from outside the solar system.

Etiquette, Continued

Alexander von Humboldt held his fork in his left hand while explaining that the quantity of heat received by a body from another depends on the relative position of the two bodies.

Two women in long white gowns came in. We had to strip naked and walk slowly in front of them. When it was my turn I felt dizzy.

From Kosmos or Physical Description of the Universe

Alexander von Humboldt drew lines isodynamic, isoclinal, isothermal, then followed them hand in hand with Aimé Bonpland. If only Napoleon were not invading Russia. He walked on the surface heavy with grief where the barometer reduced to sea level read the same. Here the rock beds had the same dip and the magnetic needle the same inclination to the plumb line. His head related to zones of force having equal angles, equal pressure, equal tension, all edges equally foreshortened.

Physical Description of Sexual Intercourse, Continued

Alexander von Humboldt did not trust the soundings of navigators who had voyaged there before him and with such apparent ease.

This Is To Say

The only effective defense against the insects was to wave one's arms and slap one's body.

Physical Description of Sexual Intercourse, Continued

To cure injuries caused by the sting-ray, you must find a woman willing to strip and urinate into the wound. For the sake of completeness it must be stated that, as there are hardly any women here except peasant prostitutes, this cure more often than not leads to a particularly virulent kind of syphilis.

The ballad presents a romantic or heroic theme in impersonal form.

Beethoven's loneliness was terrible and complete.

Explanation

Muscular fatigue has been ascribed to the irritating effects on the nerve plates of an excess of sarcolactic acid and extractives.

Posthumous Writings

Blue trousers are cooler than white. If the Aztecs had only known that their omens were comets, harmless wanderers in space. O to be on top of a mountain. Someone might again ask: why do you run across the world? To compare your grass with other grass? The icy pole or point of the greatest cold no more corresponds with the terrestrial pole than does the word "promise." Everything dissolves in menstrual blood.

Volcanoes, Concluded

"Alexander von Humboldt is a spy," said Napoleon.

Pretending to attack the insurgents, Iturbide secretly cultivated their friendship and, in 1821, entered into an agreement, the Plan of Iguala or of the Three Guarantees: unity among Mexicans of all classes, the sun's powers limited by a constitution, and protection of the aberration constant.

Reference

Aimé Bonpland died in 1858, in Borja, near the Brasilian border. On the way to the graveyard, a drunken peasant took offense that the corpse would not return his greeting and ran a dagger through it.

Physical Description of Motion, Concluded

They hanged Macuilxochitl in Coyoacan. They also hanged Pizotzin, the King of Culhuacan. And they fed the Keeper of the

Black House to their dogs. And three wise men of Ehecatl were devoured by their dogs. They had come to surrender. They arrived bearing their painted sheets of paper. There were four of them, and only one escaped. The other three were overtaken, there in Coyoacan.

Alexander von Humboldt felt weak and feverish. He remained flat in bed, and his horizon, meridian and prime vertical stayed in a constant and definite position. His thought was in the last fraction of its diurnal arc, preparing to leave the horizon.

Slowly, slowly we walked through the streets, seeming to glide above the ground. A procession of girls in long white gowns. Slowly we lifted our knees and let our feet touch the ground with the tip of our toes. We walked as if carried by a cool wind. On both sides of the street, crowds of people were cheering, showering us with flowers. I saw a procession of boys, also in white gowns, approach from the other side as we mounted the temple steps toward the priest in the white robe, toward the great black stone, toward the flaming sun.

Physical Description of Sexual Intercourse, Concluded

When the explorer does not encounter any object, his mind spirals off into space.

Flesh which is object for no subject becomes disturbing and uncommunicable.

Rigor mortis is due to coagulation of myosinogen and paramyosinogen by fibrin ferment, forming a cloth of myosin. Sarcolactic acid and acid potassium phosphate are also generated in considerable quantity after death, and probably aid in the process of coagulation.

III

A Form of Doubt

A sentence has to do with. Most problems occur in part III, I say, perhaps I should try to avoid it. The cat on the sill. The sun lighting up the tips of his fur. The imperatives of narration, you say, your back against the window. One thing to get Amy sick in bed, thick smell of camomile, defenseless, smile, eddy and swirl without turn signals or traffic cops, a mile a mismatch. This morning even the egg in its cup self-sufficient, waiting to be spoken to, the napkin blue. I like to balance my chair on its hind legs. Amy might say that once, seeing Ada asleep, she was suddenly frightened of the passage of time across our bodies, frightened to touch Ada's feathery hair, shifting cloud beds, fingers adrift.

I am old enough to like a landscape gone to weeds. Notched yardstick. Like Amy, a woman of a certain age, a certain armor, all cotton turtlenecks. The mornings less promising now, reefs surface and shallows, a pain in the stomach, a fluttering like a flock of birds, of course I'm anxious, these scattered notes, scribblings in margins, scraps of paper. It is November, still warm. The radiator on regardless. The reason I don't know. Columbus sent out parties to the gold regions of Cibao. The sun's heat made solid. If you turned around you could perhaps see the dog I hear barking. If you turned around you could see the glare on the window. If you turned around you could at least see the window. A character on my hands, you say. Another body, solid. This room perfect except for your cautious look, expecting rain before proximity, I realize the color blue does not mean extremes of heat and cold to everyone. Eyes can be too bright, can, like too precise a set of circumstances, fade the subject back into the negative. Not mine, of course, which are rather getting weaker, blurring distinctions out of perception. So I run upstairs, downstairs, from room to room, look for things on my desk, on the floor, out of breath, and the days go by.

A frame, you say. Of action. Amy could slap her body against insects, hold her fork in her left hand while she explains to her friends Victoria and John that the quantity of heat received by a body from another depends on their relative position. On the page. No, you say. And why Mexico? Though you know my obsession with the Conquest. The use of sentences in. My immigrant fixation, you concede. More, I say. The great encounter with the unpredicted. Extremes of otherness. Who—or which—won't fit our frame. Of reference, you say. Yes, or window. I could still have Amy tense and relax her leg muscles in such a way that they take her to the Zocalo or Alameda, you say. Let her look at the ahuehuetl trees, the Old Market, at women sitting on crates next to baskets of fruit, the folds of their skirts, flies, mounds of crumpled paper and rotten produce, colored awnings, men leaning against walls, eyes hidden under hat-brims, sour smell of pulque. The Cathedral. The Palacio Nacional.

But I am walking in a different city. Without purpose, stop and look up at the statues for lasting visions and, always eccentric, walk on. Federal Triangle and Judiciary Square. Roar of traffic. Island. Cross on red. The White House in a white fog. An eye on Southern neighbors. In the family, as it were: he wants them to cry uncle. A sidewalk is a narrow location in history. A sentence. Bracketed choice, lost vote, and what did I expect. Pennsylvania Avenue before the rain, the pigeons under the eaves of the Archives scream their heads off, the succession of night and day, cardboard Presidents along the street, I can have my picture taken with him, now also with Prince Charles and Princess Di, all of Washington discussing the right way to curtsey, the price of her jewels not important, only that of Ortega's eyeglasses, Daniel Ortega Saavedra, president of Nicaragua, exorbitant. Figures scurry toward the subway, the force of gravity or habit, bluish shadows before rain, the stripes of my blouse have run out in the wash, blue like Amy's dream of Ada, turbulent winds, subterranean fissures, the blue plumage prized by the Aztecs for funeral attire. I wanted to keep a log of my steps, downbeat of the body, weight rolling from heel to toes, as they carry me outward from the centers of powers, to where the buildings size down to warmer brick, a foghorn from the river, a dog lifts its leg against a parking meter, a boy on a bicycle, women with shopping bags, and how tired I am by the time I get there, no part of my body comfortable, certainly not the feet.

The weather is changing. Loss by radiation in excess of. I scrutinize the form and color of clouds, the trace of wind in the sycamores, flock of sparrows, the depth of shadows for clues of tomorrow's verbs. The delay is fatal. What has happened to today? The color grey, not blue.

Now then, you say. Amy could hold a teacup. "Why is she not in bed?" asks little Isabel, leaning against her mother's chair the way she had leaned in the half-open door to the sick-room. Amy puts her roll down on her plate, her teeth marks in the butter. Even when they were classmates John never minded that she listens without tilting her head to the side, without pretending to enjoy being instructed when the market calls for even exchange. Victoria pours tea, steaming, into the cups. "Why is she not dead?" asks little Isabel. Amy leans back in her chair. As long as she skirts certain areas, pulls a skirt over, yes, that one, which exercises a powerful influence on the quantity of humidity in the atmosphere. Jilted is an oldfashioned word. Another sugar, she says, sure.

John talks of his Humboldt biography. A mirror to discover things about himself. Amy wants to ask which, the sex, the urge to connect, but prefers to think of a window, opposite direction, lean out, not thrown back on herself. A window, a lens gathering language, a focus to burn. Conjunctions and connotations. She touches John's arm as if to apologize for these disagreements and remembers Ada's hair with her fingertips, how many more people in every scene.

Words get thinner, my hair, and slower, out of breath climbing the stairs. Leaden legs. I take longer to think, sudden starts, headaches, harder to talk to people, out of it, always. Resistance. Inkstains. Bottom of the page. The sun invades, a blinding glare, my Jade Garden, my room in green and black, including the cat, as designed as the city surrounds, and lacking my anchor, Keith's breath in the room, the next room, somewhere in the house, all landmarks disappear, the sun horizon extends all the way around my aching eyes. Adrift on a table, triangular, black, bare no more, mine for a 3-week shift on government money, implicated, bags of groceries, time on my own. Sleeves rolled up to indicate hard work, avert suspicions of imposture. Not a real writer, it would have to come easier, not this despair as I suck the pen, the pencil, words on loan, charged, not enough, too many, too used. Can I use them over again? Ideas in the air. Nouns by the hour. Churchbells. Cackling bluejay. The cat not interested.

Isogrammatical lines connecting the mean incidence of comparable parts of speech map the discourse of the world, I say. Against their average, extremes of sense and absence create the pleasure of fragments. Break the silence and pick up the pieces to find a cluster of shards which catches light on the cut and the next day too.

But the claims, you say, the enormous claims of continuity. Of course, I'm scared, and raised the way I was, the way women of my age were, I try to oblige, glue the shards, spread my legs, this time for balance, chemical, but also rebel, assemble my forces and start a zigzag march on the rules of grammar. Lightning speed. Fire truck heading North. A sentence that allows for confusion. Centrifugal. The troops inexperienced, poorly equipped, no auxiliaries from outside the solar system, but the momentum now pushes the sentence beyond what should be its end, and I don't give a damn even though I know that, if there is advance, it's only because the earth is pulled in the opposite direction under my pen.

Can you see me, the explorer, rebel, aggressive stranger, tottering, uncertain, the would-be conqueror come after the others across the sea, wave after wave beating against the naked shore, naked page, naked alphabet. And into. Obscene desire. Understood as treachery, the rivers run through the land in cahoots with invaders, like the heart, like women, allowing penetration, Potomac and Pocahontas swell with the tide. Captain John Smith explored the river in 1608, you say, possibly as far as it falls, past the villages of Tauxemont and Acoughtant, the first to reach the river's navigable head, and later canal plans as far inland as the Ohio.

Reminders of an older power, the presence of the river in the soil, the elevation on which the Capitol is built, terraces carved out by the Potomac in a prehistoric age when, you say, augmented by glaciers in the north, it rushed with great force and volume through the widening channels. It is not the past I mean, but the water, even underground, its instability and challenge, or running through the pipes. Finding substantial footing is a difficult engineering problem for any government. More so here in Washington. Crass roots. The marshy ground makes huge subfoundations necessary for public buildings, to distribute their weight over the entire population, crass struggle, the logic of rubbers, immense piles driven deep below Pennsylvania Avenue. Beneath the Archives, you say, huge pumps must operate to safeguard the national memory from old Tiber Creek, its surreptitious seepage through the concrete.

In the course of paving the streets of Mexico City, John could tell his old pal Amy, on August 13, 1790, the construction crew dug up an enormous statue of the Great Goddess Coatlicue with her skirt of serpents. There is a legend that the Viceroy afterwards tried to hug his knees in his sleep, approaching a circle as much as aging closes in on childhood until the serpent strikes the fault in the curve. But had the statue carried to the Royal and Pontifical University of Mexico as a monument of American antiquity. The Viceroy Revillagigedo.

Setting, you say. The sun fuzzy and shapeless, doesn't apply. Too early. Out the window, red haze. Already hot. Sedative. Filtered light. Fierce, rippling heat. Amy could hold on to her empty teacup, you say, although the few leaves at the bottom do not promise much future, a dancer's life is short, some other reason then, also for wrapping her legs around those of her chair. Dazed. Drops of sweat on her upper lip. Salty. Swarms of butterflies lift off the eucalyptus, the poppies and bromelias bright as pain. She has trouble breathing. Does a big body, the weight not evenly distributed, need more air, stash it up for another swirling flight, muscles contracting to bring her close to Alexander von Humboldt and other spare parts? Or words start up, perpetual motion, a multitude of impulses, faint, elusive, a twittering inside the skull, then sweating it out in a million small adjustments to the plumb line.

A descent into the body, seven caves, seven canyons, and can she come back the same, you ask. A foreign country, increase of heat and motion. Her foot falters on unfamiliar ground, not aloof, not in a car or on horseback, the feel of displacement. Plums drop from the trees, the pulse in her left wrist racing, the roar of traffic, how do you explain it? The Spanish for plain is llanura. She would stretch her expectations over the lake, but it is not there. No longer lacustrine, Mexico City, memory seeped out of reach along with the lake, salt marshes all that is revealed to the sleepless. Coming up for air. Ada's dreams of drowning. A catalogue of wind conditions. Work. The dorsal ridge of the Sierra Madre, the grain of experience. To bring forth. Travail, the hard work of travel, the equinox westward. Goes out expecting trouble, goes out prepared. A Spanish translation of the French Declaration of the Rights of Man by Antonio Narino. 1794. Red stones. She walks too fast. The rest is easy. I draw lines to Amy's body and follow them into the skin of an Aztec girl. She knows what is going to happen. Scissors cut paper. Her place fixed, while language, however afterward, has no limits, I am Cortés, the ruthless, I am everything I've ever read or written or thought, without substance or solar constant, without even gravity. I misplace words as well as things. On your desk, you say. No, I say, in the sentence. And missed opportunities, you say. With abandon. Mesa means table as well as plateau. The longer the movement grows collision.

A disturbed equilibrium, you say, that requires development and complications, resolution. John's role in Amy's broken engagement. The messengers were painted with chalk. Years earlier, John might go on, Charles III had given the university a collection of plaster casts of Greek and Roman statues. The Coatlicue was placed among them. But not for long. A goddess without a head. Two jets of blood rise from her neck in the form of snakes, rise from a ghastly necklace of severed heads and hands. Nothing human about her except breasts and those only partly visible. The *doctores* of the university had bad dreams. Some held the statue would enourage idolatry among the Indians, others, that its presence among the classical ideals was an affront to the idea of beauty. It had to be reburied.

Beauty, Amy might think. How it webs its feathery hair over the nothingness, how crucial not to get tangled, the blue of Victoria's blouse, how it blew northward, intense misunderstandings like toothmarks on the apple so it seems harmless, not a foam of knowledge and death on her tongue, startled off balance, everything large, suddenly, the mole on John's earlobe huge and mocking in its unimportance, only Ada in place, distributes the weight of her body over the entire surface of her absent look.

Amy's self as precarious as my own in spite of her great archeptypal mass of body and cigar. Volatile alter egotism. I've smoked too many successful Egyptian campaigns. Stuck in my craw. Alternate spells of coughing. Where did I put the dictionary? Big body and bad habits: being elsewhere in her head, the clouds, warmer climates, Montezuma's biceps shortens and bulges with caution as he lifts his cup, an ill-timed earthquake, or Filene's bargain basement, too far North, not where she now walks, you say, across the large entrance hall of the Museum, the Patio, round like a sea horizon, she can nearly scan the slow turning again, stress versus emphasis, the planetary spin, herself a marker which the Foucault pendulum is bearing down on. This rhythm that the earth imprints on our bodies, a force beyond control, sweeps her off while she still tries to track it in words. She breaks out in a sweat, you say. Victoria beside her, pulls her to a bench, an oasis of succulents, shade, Shakespeare sonnets, caesura. If there are no strangers, the husband must wrap his finger in a white cloth which is torn into bloody bits and distributed to the priests. This does not cause pain. Only poverty. Average US household income rose 1.7% in 1982, but fell 3.8% for households headed by women. In 1984, women working full time earned 64% of what men earned. They are expected to earn 75% by the year 2000. The weakness passes out of her legs, splash of the fountain cool, she burps, connotations clear, the intensity of the earth's magnetic force decreases from pole to equator. At least not Alexander von Humboldt's symptoms. Not all of them.

Old friend John, you say, with tickets and smile, no sense of pause and effect, he is so excited that Antonio de Léon y Gama had had time to write down a description of the Coatlicue before she was reburied. A description, he says, which wasn't published until 1804 in Rome, in an Italian translation, and imagine: Alexander von Humboldt read it. He asked to be allowed to examine the statue as soon as he arrived in Mexico. The authorities granted permission, dug up the statue, let Humboldt look at it and, when he was satisfied, buried it again.

No Great Goddess under the White House. Dense packs. Not the season for cherry blossoms. Though remains of three layers of Indian settlements two miles off. Numerous artefacts, you say, 2000 skeletons, including two of the largest skulls ever found. Growing skill changes ideas of simplicity. What if we move the metaphor not across a stable field of resemblances, but across an area itself shifting, discontinuous? I underestimated. At the time of Captain Smith's visit, about 100 warriors lived on this spot. A wide variety of wahoo, arrowwood, also called burning bush. Charred post holes show that the village later, you say. When the dance was loveliest, when song was linked to song, when the meridians converged toward the pole. Adolescent sex. Sudden desires. The Spaniards killed the celebrants, the Iroquois harried the tribes in the lower Bay. Manifest destiny. A soap stone quarry with vessels on Connecticut Avenue. Down in the valley was strangely beautiful. Rows of new apartments.

Only last year the United States honored and buried an unknown soldier of the Vietnam War in Arlington National Cemetery. Since advanced medical technology has made possible identification of the dead from even small fragments of bodies, it took the government over 10 years to find an unknown Vietnam War soldier to represent the 58,012 servicemen killed.

The pottery of the tidewater Indians was almost entirely utilitarian, you say, with rudimentary decoration, usually geometric patterns, confined to the neck and rim. Hard work as a substitute for dread. A theory of rhyme, of dressing the reasons. Less aggressive than the neighboring Iroquois. Often the pot was shaped within a net, and the impression left on the clay or partially smoothed off. So that this net of streets stretches not only horizontally, intending the infinite, but also in vertical repetition, a treatise on optics heads back to cords stretched over finger tips and pressed into the clay in Anacostia, then called Nacothtant or Acoughtank and not safe from strangers. Clean bones. Phonemes Algonquian. All gone now. Need for balance. Geometric compulsion pushing outward and inward, forward and backward like any sentence, cheerful self-sufficiency until small-pox, spirituous liquors and abridgment of territory.

The year of digressions, you say, setting the house in order, sorting perspectives from interpretation from fabrication from craving for truth. But I have already taken off my shoes. Moving closer to the impossible object, feet against the cat's flank, soundboard for his purr. Pick up a plot where I never left it? The Goddess is huge. Amy was forewarned, I could say. But nearly square. Stands there. It is not the gruesome details, the serpent skirt, the serpent squirts of blood where the face should be, the necklace of severed heads and hands. But stands there. Huge. As if always. Absence of face, staring. Too large. Menacing. Listen to her silence. Here, the still center, not in Amy's patterns, perfect pitch black, precise curve thither, precise shade of color the world habitable. The *doctores* had been right. This figure does not speak to our desolation, anguish, glands or secret wishes, not with the breath of this language or that. An absent eye. Plumed blood, blue serpent, gave birth to the moon and her four hundred brothers, hearts torn from the chest, terror of the sun.

Forewarned, but not forearmed, I could say. Amy's mysteries gravity and movement. A walk as if carried by a cool wind. Space between words. Not divine voids grafted on human intersections. Though tracing the between extends the beat of silence behind. She has not even seen an absent scapegod bleed in a golden chalice, has not eaten His body while young boys murmured in Latin. Mercurochrome and antihistamines. Mailboxes, their lovely blue. But only in the dark can one see the speed of light. Ticket windward, a kite, color of alarm in her cheeks, out of kilter, the script gone up in smoke. Hazardous to your health to let a statue hit you. Pre-emptive first strike lucky. The iron hot.

Victoria has moved off, clacking heels, the weight of the body resting on the ball of the toes, not distributed equally over the entire sole, uncertain rhythm, the pauses dominant as in writing. But John's impatience tugs at Amy, shuffles his weight from foot to fetish, image of eagerness, words dammed up, pressure mounting, wanting to pour out.

The cars stop and start, towards Pennsylvania Avenue, the light changes yellow to red to green, light drizzle, waves of traffic, eddies around columns and cornices. Disoriented as in any sea, dizzy is not the question, vague terms, waves, wind chill, mail truck still on the mall, mass of papers, stares behind glass, Capitol Hill, a good place to think about power and small print. Drift from calamity to calamity, phantom whip and backlash, flying Dutchmen, illegal aliens, adjective based on fugitive, smells fishy, eyes full of alarm, shifting fears, I spear a squint at territory to the south, eyes cocked for conquest, not, this time, of Mexico.

A boy sails by on a skateboard, hoard of red berries on a tree whose name I don't know, already farther south, a mild November day, moon in the afternoon, hazy. "Life has become too complex." Not only the leaders of the people are confused. No simple binary fun, no grid of letters and numbers, meridians converge, cluster of motives, lines curl, names, pressure points, tangle of clues which allow perhaps to deduce, but remain guesses, shadowy, inflation inward, the compass needle turns from North to South, approaching graspable as a stroke of light tears open a building, on Edgar Chamorra and two other Contras, rehearsing a press conference with CIA advisors:

"Wrong. Your aim is *not* to overthrow the Sandinistas. It is to create conditions for democracy."

"Next question: where have you been getting money?"

Three helpless Nicaraguans.

"Say your sources want to remain confidential."

Dissolves as I try to be sure. Windows bang shut, brain capacity limited, bad memory, leaking pen that blots out my notes. Advanced not-understanding. Semiofficial spermicides. Political hay. Silence on silence, piles of plates in the sink, truth-tables and easy-chairs, records in libraries and contradictory genealogies. Not all responsibilities can be shirked. Or make our flashes of desire reach beyond the clothesline. Real body, its short . . . and the dirty dishes.

The reader's expectations, you say. Think of the weather, I say, its changes, a form free of forecast in spite of. And if it resembles is why we find it.

That's the way you are, John breaks out with unexpected vehemence, always held in, even with friends, why don't you say something.

He's not exactly Latin himself. Held in. Of course. Amy has had to be. Flood warnings become second nature. Ropes to be kept near in case of need. Still, her terror that all vegetation might get stifled, nothing but glazed volcanic sand up to the limits of perpetual snow.

She would like to talk about Ada, her crossing the equator, Egyptian campaign, flags moving up and down the mast. At the same time annoyed that she still wants John's approval as in their college days. Why was she so eager to seize on his wife's projects, texts into Spanish, body to Mexico, wasn't it all ranklings from twenty years back? Hard to wrest one's independence from the force of gravity or gender patterns. O John, she knows she ought to be just a good sport, intimate, but not too, especially no claims, a well-behaved guest.

But Victoria, you say. Easy confidences, soft couch to sink into, her hair feathery like Ada's, ruffled black. Though her enthusiasm, when anything would seem too precise a label, too heavily inked. Sudden grass fire, quick flames, the sentences break rank and flee right into the smoke. No, Amy was not proving a point, outlines blur, an ache to press against, at one time John perhaps if it hadn't been Henry. Had she said that?

Now Victoria comes back toward the Coatlicue, toward Amy and John, then hesitates, veers off, does she sense the tension between them? Amy listens to the definite clacks, foreshortened weight of the body, more high heels here than in a New York museum. But John hasn't changed from the old days, has again taken up the thread of his lecture.

Her career has run its gamut: Goddess, demon, monster, masterpiece. She has changed her nature on the way from temple to museum, is, as it were, in a foreign climate here, no longer a crystallization of power, but an episode in the history of religion. But is she really? He is nearly triumphant. Is it not impossible to pass her by?

Yes, Amy admits, I can see her smeared with blood, and the dogs barking. In the Great Temple of Tenochtitlan. Stone mass scented with Copal. Copulation? False cognate. I don't know if I'm attracted or repelled, she says. Afraid, I think.

Now John is pleased: I knew you'd feel her power. Don't you think it is at best equivocal to call this a work of art, to call any work of ancient civilizations that? A goddess, a mystery that paralyzes.

The serpent's eye, says Amy. Ceaseless. Does he expect some special reaction from her, news from the mother country, a test of sexuality? She remembers his old "what-does-this-remind-you-of?" tease of her ignorance before he would reveal his discoveries. Involuntary muscles. Slow, but protracted contraction in the viscera. The serpents writhing over the void, writing to cover up lack of identity, of substance. Or with speed. Henry racing his car, and she dying in gear beside him. Another photo she had removed, much earlier, her hair blown, wings in the air, filling it up, excitement bending the light rays out of their course, still assuming participation in government rather than abridged desire, her mind rotating on its axis no milky way or wet garden. Pull back from reality, but pull it down with her as she falls into the sentence. Suspended, she thinks better of it, and the highway, at eighty, look out where you in the long run. And how did that work out? you ask. In the open. Desperate conflict in which both parties managed to avoid defeat in spite of an ill-timed earthquake. Not your usual baby carriage, shopping cart and divorce court, but, in the soberness of morning, she hears a door close and draws back the curtains on couplets, common measure and the garbage can. Sits on the page, legible, and has learned the art of questioning. Finger to the bone for an always new form and discontent. Or throws birdseed between the word for word, red fire truck, a walk to the post office, and how about a bicycle.

Close, too closely connected the linked arms and events on the make, in the place of empathy and identification where you walk up the steps into your own open and welcome. I've never liked mirrors, I say, and why don't you want to look at the cracks between shards?

Amy sees lines of force go out from the goddess, link Victoria and John and their child, link Ada and Paul, and the way their hair is braided together and toward her with the warm illusion of friendship, yet breaks off, link fence, leaving a white area around her, snow crystals packed tight. Can she walk across on her hands?

She takes herself too seriously, if hard, her coffee black. Victoria's smallness makes her all bulk, fat baby again, shift it from foot to other measures, her bag from shoulder to hold on to the museum floor plan as if it were the key to the scriptures.

She has to be square, says Victoria:

The four corners of the sky
of the earth
four stakes driven into the ground
to mark the cornfield for cultivation

America is the fourth dimension. The fourth continent, its culture ruled by the figure 4: Every god had four aspects, every space four directions, every reality four faces. But the Europeans did not accept the challenge. They insisted on conquest, imposed their triad: 3 times, 3 ages, 3 persons in one god. So the Goddess must be a demon, and woman, man's negative mirror.

What a speech, John puts his arm around his wife, warmly masking his need to hold on as words come loose, an unfastened woman, panic of separation, the station empty as the train pulls out and smokes the mirror. Climatic distribution of erections and brain capacity. Amy thinks of a taunt, jokingly, so as not to hurt them both, or would she like to? Dart a bit of poison, twist the penknife under their touching toenails? As she would like to hurt Ada. How many times has she dreamed the dream of the big blue bird? The bird at the bus stop, the beach, the bank, the Mexican border, the breach of promise. Alternation of flight and perching. Blue feathers like a deep sky. She stands stunned. Alliteration reinforces fear of flying. Legs open, a sharp thrill of thirst. Runs, runs, till feathers brush fingertips, wings spread, beat out of her reach. Then, suddenly, the gun.

Everything in life happens in the past, though not always as far back as Freud would have us believe, and what has not happened between John and her stretches between them. Impulses, muffled like voices in the museum, don't travel half the distance between statues. There are no windows. Nothing has grown but hair and fingernails and words, words, color bleached by paper except for the black fur of the cat. Panic of cut-off from the environment, edges, vague, into fiction and fantasy, a sea inviting voyage, discovery and even commerce, barges of spice and fruit.

The heater fan fills my sleep with a noise as white as traffic, as the ocean, as crowds with cameras. The props of the city askew, the diagonals have risen out of the horizontal plane, buildings lean at dangerous angles, held up only by the Reflecting Pool. What if the water is diverted? The people are where my body doesn't reach, where are they, I cry, strange time, before sunrise, and in this storm, I cry, that sweeps a flood of red leaves from the trees, or is it blood, let it be a dream that stars are at war and the full moon falls on Sunday.

Justice is so precise an impossibility, says the President, that we can only step up surveillance of the border between ideas and action. He has never set foot on the land, all his life on horseback or inside his purring car, a couple of feet above the ground, now wings to fly to the summit, flight of ideas where there are none, spotlights in many colors, corolla, ex machina.

A promise of suspended sentences and questions. Language will let us off, every time, lenient, or will it when we advocate "use of violence (to) neutralize carefully selected targets, such as court judges, police and state security officials." A training manual for Nicaraguan rebels. Made in USA.

Not a nightmare, not just an outcrop of fear. Verb to disturb and vertigo. A court judge's face blackened with smoke. Another still standing with blood streaming over his coat as from a bottle. Harbor this for me. Edgar Chamorro was not happy, an ex-Contra now, not happy to take credit for the mining. "Why did the CIA not give us the money and let us actually do the job?" I don't know the half of it, the long and short, or the answer. Open the windows. A yellow dog lopes sideways along the sidewalk. Creases on my skin from the net of sleep, of the past, does it shape me like a clay pot, dense matter for practical tasks, and the pattern no grid, no boxed-in squares, too many subordinate clauses, threads unforeseen, Montezuma, the Reichstag fire, Napoleon's retreat, adjectives receptive to mother's death. The vast twilight zone slips around the earth as the latter turns on its axis. Mind a participle by stretches across distant dust, now part of my body till I die or lose all memory.

You say, if this is narrative. Of prepare, I say. What? you ask. A quote, I say. Why don't you just lean out the window and look at the maples, red, battling with fall, that same yellow dog, the government employees hurrying to the Archives. Never mind the yellow dog, you say. Look straight across the vacant lot: The future is female like most allegories. There she sits with her open book, pulling the next sentence down into her marble weight. And I'm lucky it's her. A bit farther West I'd be facing the closed book of the Past, layers of sediment, irrevocable residue, piled up in periods, not just in the Archives, concrete on top of the marshland, the shifting, soggy land we've tried so hard to tame we forget it is there. And is it? Haven't we got the better of it? Trapped in soliloquies we cannot transcend, Morton Salt Girls, in nets of interpretations spread like the city in quadrants and grids, centrifugal, centripetal, cheerfully schizophrenic.

No tear in the flesh, kids misplaced among the virtualities, and that even language might desert me, might scatter into the night while I still sit at my table, my place under the lamp without being able to call the words into its cone of light. Oh, I can grab my ass and throw my body backward, I've made sure no child will swim out of my howl, not this kind of blank page, mind to decipher and colonize, not even the passing illusion of plenitude and perfect communication, the baby at the breast.

And set out early when it was still morning and foggy though, as you know, I'm more at home with the night, and walked by the Memorial of the Grand Army of the Republic, by the dolphins of the Temperance Fountain—and why does Temperance carry it over Faith, Hope, Charity on the other three sides?—by General Hancock on his horse, by the Archives, by Past and Future in search of the present. Which must be tangible here, concentrated in this city, not just by dint of size. But, on the contrary, every instant operates with a view to consequence, plans and annals, conferences, even the air conditioned toward results, the future progresses on schedule. Without the aid of watches, the troop photo would be jeopardized. The government industry produces cold feet in cold war heads, on toward the promise of being in explosive charge. The frontiers to the south will be crossed ideologically. An image of success, unspoiled by bums who are kept from sleeping on the sidewalk heating grates by metal sheds built over them.

I've never seen so many representations of birth, Amy might say. Not "Virgins with Child," so much more decorous, the child at the breast, but birth itself, its blood and horror and power.

You should write about the Great Goddess.

When Amy turns her head she can smell Victoria's hair, feathery tangle, Ada would push it back with so fluttering a motion, fresh smell of shampoo.

Can't carry this tune, this Texcoco blue, she says. And no kids have tumbled out of my skirt.

Victoria clicks her tongue. You write to fill up the emptiness. Whereas once you let children run through your body you follow the umbilical cord never to return.

She had said that. Conditions of exchange: the wonders of a

language game, splice of life, blue feathers and yellow beak against loss by radiation exceeding the daily quantity of heat received. And maybe barren, narrow, carriage return stuck. But there is no escape. Words. Lines. Sentences send it about most. Push against borders, keep walls at a distance, if only by an inch. Language its own obstacle. Not just the body. But the meridians continue to encircle the earth.

Some decisions were made for me by my big body, says Amy, to the clink of icecubes. A shortcut. A habit of weight. In touch with the planet by sheer gravity. Moving with it, even too fast. Not the lightness of distance, objectivity. Connected. Weigh your words, heft, lift, live them. Writing and walking, the form already there, in the space, a matter of finding rather than making. No parking. Not transparent. Not making the words disappear into their reference.

And the sting of the incomplete in each word, insufficient, the work never done, finger to the bone, not enough. Pointing beyond, leaning into between, each word a vector, versification of estrange. Sometimes a sentence in wishes she could knit sweaters, build furniture, bake bread, have a child.

With the earth overpopulated, says John, children are an indulgence as much as writing poems.

Amy doesn't rise to the dig, no case of bristle, still thinks arrangement of gaps, a sentence and sewn, two words at just the right distance that the spark flies. Or two bodies. A matter of betweens.

You don't think collision is necessary?

As much as collusion. Like between you and old Henry.

A wink, a sudden laugh, relief. Now John can ask:

I wonder what would have happened if Henry hadn't walked out on you?

What does it matter what would? Combinations infinite. A sentence knows—shows—its own errors, space to go astray, and the cat amazed. Any person is opposite. Ada's blue not like my own Monday. Sometimes not certain that the sun will rise in the east, red, a red letter I wrote her today because it's Sunday though it parades with a more resonant name here.

I was thinking, interjects Victoria, that the only times I have felt really at home in my body were when I was nursing. The child is indeed my indulgence. In the religious sense. Otherwise, you know, I'm even shy about being naked.

Your Catholic upbringing, says John.

His protestantism hasn't served him any better. The way he used to hold on to his clothes before experimenting inside. Careful, Amy, before the equinox travels farther to the west, a crisis of brazen and no one there at all.

Still, laughs Victoria, in spite of the nuns, I was a happy little girl whereas I am not sure John had any childhood at all.

John's early screams, reading what traumas and terrors, Amy can't shed any light on them, not even reflected, a moon with distortions, call it clouds or stopping to puzzle. We talked future, she says, not everybody's unhappy childhood, comparing local times all around the globe.

Do you remember, says John, and Amy apprehensive. Ingrained time loop. Do you remember how I used to tell my recurrent dream that Emily Dickinson was dead, and how mad you got? You claimed I tried to kill her again and again?

How do you like Washington, you ask, and I say too clean, too stinking rich, too much marble, granite, limestone, too many domes, columns and porticos, spare parts, too vertical, too strenuously erect, too visible the presence of government, the constant reminder that I am implicated. I am doing my best just to walk through it though already I think of the way you happen to open a book and are slowly, step by step, drawn into its make-belief world. Until, at the end, you suddenly fall, like Lionel Johnson off the barstool or what's-his-name out of the window because St. Paul's sermon went on and on, no way to get out except by falling, asleep and thence to his death.

Maybe it isn't good for you to look at an allegorical statue day after day, you say. What happened to the yellow dog? Did you not claim you were good at measuring distances?

A matter of friction, I say, between me and the outside, between me and the words, that keeps it interesting, throws off sparks like the sexual researches of a child, and here, as in political life, it is the lacunae in the answers that censor the inquiry, deflect it into questions of protocol, the "order of things," too many mirrors.

The granite shiny on the Vietnam Veterans Memorial, reflects my body as I look, the names cover it, make believe I'm one of them, will be, no injuries natural, no way to back off for a long view. Held to it, to the cry of I died, black gash, hearts torn from the chest, blood spilled to feed the sun.

Did I need to let you take me up the Washington Monument to know that it's a vertical world, power in the hands of men, a constant masturbation? At least it does not pretend to be in honor of *God on high* like the church towers I used to climb, step by worn stone step up spiral staircases which, turn by turn, screwed the roofs into a dizzy depth I felt in my knees, in every muscle, striated fiber and connective tissue, in the wind gone out of my lungs, centrifugal force. Here, of course, elevators, lack of effort as if to demonstrate that the intensity of the earth's magnetic force decreases with height.

Dizzy? you mock. There is no insight without height and fear of, no perspective or overview.

I lean into it, city pushed into its map. November sun, colors muted by exhaust, except for the glistening ribbon of the Potomac. Edges hedged with haze, gray-green. There, to the East, I can nearly imagine I see the sea I came across, pushing against the wind, late particle of the waves of explorers and conquistadors, can nearly imagine I see the will to conquer turn and veer south with that low plane passing overhead, southward, slow it seems from here.

The important distance, I say, may be down rather than up. Orpheus, Odysseus, Faust—

OK, you say, go live in the subway.

But you know that erections don't last, except in rigor mortis, the ground a problem, the water underneath. Cracks and fissures in the psychology of standing tall and hanging tough. Crisis brought about by decrease in temperature. 1° Celsius for every 160 meters. After 3200 meters the souls freeze, stiff with superiority, bewailing the hard fate of having to be hard. And the dreams of conquest topple or, given the proximity of water, wobble, wilt, viscous, white, spilling over the ground.

You admit the water's surreptitious presence under the concrete, the remains of the cypress swamp from M Street to 17th and K, the marshy ground. It was the 1854 resurvey, you say, that revealed the necessity of introducing a subfoundation of concrete under the Washington Monument to distribute the weight over a much larger area than originally planned. Something to be "dealt with." All that does not take place between the vertical and horizontal.

Water in any form, swelling the sponge in the sink, lapping into a poem, the river's abrupt narrowing at Key Bridge, the violence of its torrents and gorges, precipitous banks towards the Falls. And bridges. I like to feel the vectors of river and traffic at right angles, the pull of forces, and the reflections wave and ruffle across the grid scheme just as my sleep takes pleasure in what I censor and sew into the dream egg and, thus masked, allow to come up again, suitable for daylight, for the time of habit, of scales over the eyes. Three weeks in this city, not enough to develop the common blindness, still excited by the slug on the sidewalk, a little girl runs for the bus, scarf streaming behind her, and not used to my new glasses either which I need for reading now, but I look up from the book and all is blurred and dizzy, the plane passing overhead, low, ready to land, more blurred than its reflection in the Potomac, and right below me now a barge, sluggishly moving upstream, rusty-looking, nearly the color of sand, its cargo, even the white of the wake rusty in the muddy brown, taste of blood in my mouth, gums flooding the teeth or tunnels of the subway.

Friction, I say, not a moment without it, or fiction either. The window needs wiping. The hot water pipes clang. Even writing can't always envelop, can't sustain me with its order and disorder, and how is women's different from men's—"ifferent" I had typed, if it is. Slicing it this way. Mining seven different caves and canyons. Letting this city drift through polymorphous sentences, rather than follow the plots of invasions and invaders in a straight line, the female mere body, mere site of the proceedings? Like the young Indian woman Alonso de Avila seized during the Conquest. She had promised her husband, who feared he would die in battle, that she would never belong to another, and nothing could induce her to let a man near her. So she was thrown to the dogs. But if the female is also the invader, an accomplice, part of the power which tries to control the other America? The distance foreshortened with grief, not a simple ratio of two whole numbers. Grammatical revolt, syntactical subversion, a verb is a change, and the fear it will stay there, in grammar and syntax, while I sit at the edge of the Reflecting Pool, no tax on sun, the grass still so green here in November, and a little leaf of clover. Better join the next march. Or sooner. Dreams and illusions, the Pool controls the water, forcing it to be geometrical like everything else here, and why not admit it, I too hold on to the clarity of shape, the jar, the net, how else to navigate the welter, the too-much from all sides. To be open, as a book is only a book when open, naked to what cuts, open like a grid, like the streets of this city stretching outward in all directions and yet bounded at every intersection, centers unlimited, an orange in every word.

Writing is impossible, I say. The uncharted sea. A post-script to the Oedipus complex, you say. The child's repressed sexual urges sublimated in the body of the letter, a way to explore the forbidden anatomies, incestuous morphology, the white page of the mother's body, though you don't mean to denigrate my thoughts.

I don't even have thoughts, I say, I have methods that make language think, take over and me by the hand. Into sense or offense, syntax stretched across rules, relations of force, fluid the dip of the plumb line, the pull of eyes. What if the mother didn't censor the child's looking? Didn't wipe the slate clean? Would the child know from the start that there are no white pages, that we always write over a text already there? No beginnings. All unrepentant middle.

John brings up Alexander von Humboldt. It's clear his writing was compensation, obsessed with connecting, with what he couldn't do with people.

With me it's revenge, says Amy. They can laugh at this now. But also uncertainty, need to understand, to connect like your Humboldt and see what happens at the seams, the synapses. And maybe just compulsion. But, I suppose, compensation too. A sentence is made by coupling. I chew my pencil down to the lead, and Emily Dickinson must sleep in a straight line. But Victoria cuts through the archetypes, the accumulated absurdities, birth from both head and womb.

Victoria looks serious: Never mind head, heart or vagina. Think of the ground we stand on, what goes on between us and it, the subterranean turbulence. Impulses perpendicular to daylight, in any field, magnetic. Ferment. Something in motion likely to shake loose.

Your first words to me here, in your country, says Amy, were about volcanoes. The deepest rhythm, up through the sole of the foot—and may destroy you. She looks over at the heaps of rubble. Earthquakes.

Yes, says Victoria. The worst since 1973. A thousand injured in the city alone. Which is also sinking. Down, through its Spanish layers, to the teocalli and the old lake underground. You saw the Loreto Church. Santissima Trinidad leans even worse. Nothing is solid.

Behind Amy, the Venetian looking Post Office, the massive marble of the National Theater. Spared. Come through, to the other side of the quake. But two streets over, the tents, the children begging, the rows of unemployed men leaning against the fence with signs listing their skills:

Albanil	Azulejo	Mosaico y Pintura

Is it only by the fissures that we can know? Each smile its swirling hollow. But caught in circumstance, in costumes, we have to go on talking, even if we're breathless with fear, even if we know nobody is listening, words like dust whirled by the wind, and we hope they will open into the slowness of the day, the luxury of air and yet pull the contour inward.

Unsure of the ground. A hesitation and going slower. Doubts.

Hard to get lost in this city, East-West succession of numbers, total prediction. Only toward the periphery the streets start curving, intending landscape, if feebly, and the thread of letters gives out. Names, opposed to tame, scuttle the sequence, each claims unique identity, our entire attention.

The sun suddenly floods the street, the moment wonderful, luminous, I want to sing, skip along the sidewalk in spite of my age, the brick warm yellow, the baywindows glinting with all their eight sides. Daily delighted. How can a sentence make a meadow? Curled. The cat. What has happened to the black granite, the Aztec calendar? No gryphons to guard my archives. Scratchings on paper—when I should cry out as my friend Blossom does: I am indignant, she cries. Seventy years from the first rallies for women's suffrage to the 19th Amendment. Fifty years of the Equal Rights Amendment in Congress until sent to the States for ratification in 1972. What is a sentence at seventy? In seventy-two? A document in the Museum of American History. Silence about: it was not ratified. A railing keeps the stream of visitors at a carefully planned distance from the exhibits, pace and pausing subtly regulated. A sentence for thought. Blossom cries out, her umbrella purple like her clothes, the howl of the dog in the subway as he touched the rail and rolled over in pain, later, was it the same dog, snow on his fur, separate feathery flakes, like balls of mimosa.

If I stand at a window am I waiting? For my failures to make a space between them where I can stand? Shadows give shape to the light. A sentence is not why I am worried. The empty lot between my window and the Archives conforms to the dominant pattern, parallel tire marks—or are they the rakings of an excavator—and arcs of circles where the machine turned. Now that it is raining the ruts stretch shinily to the subway entrance. Some of the puddles too reflecting to show me the little circles the raindrops make. Points. In sequence. Fragments and sentences breathing sideways, in addition to forward and backward. Falling off at the end.

They hanged Macuilxochitl in Coyoacan. They also hanged Pizotzin, the king of Culhuacan. And they fed the Keeper of the Black House to their dogs. The landscape of conquest. Aberration is by no means confined to the sun. The icy pole or point of greatest power no more corresponds with the terrestrial paradise than does the word "promise." If only the President were not so hungry. Great gulfs that I try to plumb with a line, but can neither fathom nor bridge. It's done with guns now.

IV

Unpredicted Particles

1

laid down the equations
and expected obedience

or felt gradual
but all the same expected

At the wharf. The gulls were crying. And the sun going down behind the masts. Then the gulls stopped crying. It was evening, and she wore red stockings. Such little things.

> "the grammar of the word 'knows'
> is closely related to that of
> 'mastery'"

the difference
in a window
in Genoa

the window
holds my breath
the window
the breath of possibility
there where October

once we let go
of the frame
the images wave after wave

The assumptions about space and time in Maxwell's theory could not be traced back to the Newtonian laws. It seemed to follow that either Newtonian mechanics or Maxwell's theory must be false.

for all he knew in Genoa
  unsteady atoms
  with fissures toward
the ocean might end
and fall

2

imagined an encounter
that couldn't be imagined

We must distinguish at least three axes in our relation to the other. There is, first of all, a value judgment: the other is good or bad, my equal or inferior.

  reading Marco Polo
  Columbus' body started toward October

  water
  poured into the gap

        the push out of the frame
        out the window
        who are you now we're all at sea it's
        raining
        fine
        particles of

traffic of past and
incommunicable
speed swung out from the bowsprit

    distance contracting
    in the curve of
    a look
    blue pulse of sleep lapped into
    the word water

the globe
wasn't it more like
  water leaping
  a quantum nipple toward the sky
a breast
an early world

3

squints at the sun
a sailor's life
farther than
expands with words

Instead, we now say "Classical mechanics is a strictly 'correct' description of nature wherever its concepts can be applied."

still the pull still of resistance
or gravity: his eye
fell (on)
:fine *specimen*

A wind sprang up from south-east. With a laugh he said, I wouldn't at all mind having an affair with a girl like that.

the images break on the shore
images and expectations
the window
and the frame of understanding
whatever
swims out of view
you
do not match my interpretations

felt the horizon
contract
with tiredness

"the sirens are not as beautiful
as claimed"

4

in October there began
the breakdown of structures

where the word for prophecy
means also law
time becomes tangible as trouble
"they waved their lives goodbye
as the facts washed on shore"

Secondly, there is a movement toward or away from the other: I embrace the other's values or I impose my own culture on him (assimilation). It is also possible to remain indifferent.

three easy toward undressing
to see
the past
lost as new parts of speech
question
your whole
different
body

How silent she was. She would neither talk nor weep. What was he to make of such a being that leaves no more trace than a snowflake in the middle of summer?

the high speed of
smashed to probability

in love and how raw
taking captives
or naked surrender

5

putting on his boots he had expected
to walk into the mirror
                                        one of the and oldest

The window was part of it too, the window where he first saw her. But had it been at the window? Or was this just the way he remembered it later?

constant of desire
and distances that don't contract to
energy
mass
religion gold or Spanish
there where he spun his coin
so fast it left behind
the resonance
of transfer

In quantum theory the formal mathematical apparatus cannot be directly patterned on an objective occurrence in space and time. What we establish mathematically is only to a small extent an "objective fact," and largely a survey of possibilities.

                              transparency of glass and eyes
                              deceptive
                              but kin to water
                              and that I can't conceive of
                              outside my images
                              such very small
                              such very different

his heart lightly
a relation described
by the word 'between'

            tomorrow closed over
            repetition
            of water

6

amazement slung to the mast
the pronouns
billowed with outlandish reference
a rabbit out of a Genoese hat
mapped
on the infinite

the window and desire
the constant of desire
the rain runs down the
pane between experience
some fish
slip through the mesh
others have not been imagined

Thirdly, I know or do not know the identity of the other: here we obviously have an infinite gradation.

from mispronouncing fell to
hypotheses
of possession
the why and wherefore rigged
to mathematics

What was the use of these doubts? It must have been on the wharf. She was wearing laced boots, red stockings and a full, red skirt, and looked out toward the horizon as she talked.

the anchor of symmetry
way back
unable to stop
into the mirror

7

"the Cuban natives are like beasts they
do not know they live
on terra firma"

real space suddenly behind his back
three caravels aborted off
the region of smallest length

At the same time the theory must, in a certain fashion, "depict" experiences, must "mean" something in the world of phenomena.

tongue of the tide
the one tongue one
of Spanish purpose

discovery's
inevitable
there where
a window

come October
the body falls apart when looked at
measurements
spin their own memories

She did not say yes or no. She did not thank him. Back in his room he was suddenly aghast that she had accepted his offer so promptly.

that he might see
hangs by a hair
he brushed aside

dense bodies without clothes
"they know no pleasure but in women"

8

led us
a flying jib
and westward happened

But this had been at a different time. What now seemed his memory of it was really something else, part of the tangle of suspicions that had later sprung up in his head.

the window
and it's raining
I cannot see you now
the sound
against the window
no safe resemblance

would light quanta
reconcile unheard-of continents
with scripture
or a certain and cold loss
when the electron jumps an orbit

the world is
between opening our eyes

9

in October
put his foot
on a flaw in geometry

  nakedness
  another opaque

The limits of this field can never be exactly known. Only the discovery that certain phenomena can no longer be ordered by means of the old concepts tells us that we have reached the limit.

the spies drew a precise map
of the binary mutations
the distance
between memory
but the king remained mute
the information too steep too

          like you
          at the window
          not moving or
          moving only as required

          between encounter and
          transparency
          exacerbates
          the gap

10

the king of Spain too craved
jealously
the isospin
dilated saints lodged in
high wind through the pinholes

I had to
at the risk of the expected
look
into the mirror

that men can be so different
"they will die who do not understand"

To conquer, to love, and to know are autonomous, unconnected, and in some way elementary kinds of behavior.

Then too there are wedding nights when one cannot be entirely sure. There are, so to speak, physiological ambiguities.

washed past communication
broad prow into indefinite metric

there where the waves and particles
as if expecting the intruder
at the same time
uncertain
the mirror
the window

net me
silence

11

in the breakdown the right-hand spiral
whereas October came straight
at the foremast

their name means "they who explain
themselves clearly"
a nakedness
we changed to
centuries of nostalgia

These were all very slight experiences, of course, but they happened over and over again. And later they meant the opposite of what they had meant in the beginning.

the window as a boundary
the window onto
no more than swerves
remote
where are you now

curved out of the still air
yesterday
curved out of the usable air
and has no parallel where we've heaved it
the window
no more image

Providence—Paris—Washington, 1983–85

Sources

Konrad Bayer, *Der Kopf des Vitus Bering*
Douglas Botting, *Alexander von Humboldt*
Jane Bowles, *Two Serious Ladies*
Clark Coolidge, *Mine*
A. W. Crosby, *The Columbian Exchange*
Babette Deutsch, *Poetry Handbook*
Bernal Diaz del Castillo, *The Discovery and Conquest of Mexico*
H. S. Eckels, *Sanitary Science for the Undertaker*
Werner Heisenberg, *Across the Frontiers*
Alexander von Humboldt, *Kosmos, or Physical Description of the Universe*
G. Lenotre, *Napoleon*
Miguel Leon-Portilla, *The Broken Spears*
Friederike Mayröcker, *Reise durch die Nacht*
Robert Musil, *Tonka*
Octavio Paz, *Rire et pénitence*
William H. Prescott, *The Conquest of Mexico*
Ron Silliman, *Paradise*
Gertrude Stein, "Sentences"
J. W. N. Sullivan, *Beethoven*
Dennis Tedlock, ed., *Popol Vuh*
David Todd, *Professor Todd's New Astronomy*
Tzvetan Todorov, *La Conquête de l'Amérique*
Aggrippina Vaganova, *Basic Principles of Classical Ballet*
Keith Waldrop, "Puberty," from *Hegel's Family*
Frank Wedekind, *Mine-Haha*
WPA Guide to Washington, D.C.